Heartless

Susan Kiernan-Lewis

Other books by Susan Kiernan-Lewis

Reckless
Shameless
Breathless
Free Falling
Going Gone
Heading Home
Blind Sided
Rising Tides
Murder in the South of France
Murder à la Carte
Murder in Provence
Murder in Paris
Murder in Aix
Murder in Nice
The French Women's Diet
A Grave Mistake
Walk Trot Die
Finding Infinity
A Trespass in Time
Journey to the Lost Tomb
Race to World's End

Heartless

Book 4 of
The Mia Kazmaroff Mysteries

Susan Kiernan-Lewis

1

The wind sliced across the pasture. Mia sat tall in the saddle, arms held out to each side, eyes closed.

"Just feel the horse," she said. "Feel the sun on your face, the line between your heel, your hip and your shoulder."

"I am one with the horse," Jack said.

She opened her eyes and looked at him. He was digging his cellphone out of his jeans pocket.

"Stop that," she said. "You're supposed to be connecting with the horse."

"My ass is in the saddle," he said. "How much more connected can I be?"

Mia closed her legs around her horse and moved alongside Jack.

"You're not taking this seriously."

"You mean like you were yesterday when you got the giggles at the gun range?" He narrowed his eyes at her but there was a hint of amusement in them, too.

"Payback?"

"Not at all. What's your mother's new number?" He pushed a button on his phone and listened, holding up a finger to her.

"The very thought of bringing electronics into this world is a jarring imposition to the soul," Mia said, frowning.

"Hey, Jessie," Jack said into the phone, "we still on for tonight?" He nodded and gave Mia a thumbs up signal. She sighed and turned her horse back toward the barn. She hadn't had high hopes Jack would take to horseback riding.

But it would have been so nice to share this with him.

He trotted his horse up behind her. "Sorry. I just wanted to know if we could bring anything."

"Jack," she said, reining to let him catch up with her, "it's fine. I accept you as you are, as I know you struggle to do with me on a daily basis."

"Hourly."

"Fine." She grinned and he leaned across his saddle to kiss her. Mia's horse instantly kicked at Jack's horse's flank, nearly unseating Jack, who was leaning too far off his horse for the kiss.

"Whoa, partner," Mia said, laughing. "First rule of equine safety: keep the kisses safely back in the tack room."

"I was just going for a chaste peck," Jack said, holding onto his reins with both hands.

"Your 'chaste pecks' inevitably lead to more involved aerobics," Mia said. "My horse was right to shy." Mia patted her horse on the neck as if congratulating him.

When they reached the gate separating the pasture from the barn, Mia swung out of her saddle and unlatched the gate, then held it open while Jack walked through.

"Sorry, darlin', I know you wanted me to love it but I'm afraid you're stuck with Ned for the nonhuman variety of riding from now on." A committed equestrian, Ned was happy to ride any day of the week Mia was free.

Mia took Jack's reins and led both horses into the tack room, where their halters and lead ropes were hanging against the near wall.

"Don't worry about it," she said as he jumped down. "I'm sure it disappoints you that I'm not more interested in spending time in the kitchen."

"There you go."

"The appropriate answer, Jack, is 'why, not at all, pumpkin.'" She tied both horses to their wall rings.

"You want me to start calling you pumpkin?"

"*Not* what I was saying."

"Coz I think I'd put you more in the eggplant category." He put his hands on her hips and pulled her to him. Mia leaned into his kiss, feeling the warmth that always welled up between her legs and spread through her chest when he touched her.

"No time for this," she murmured into his neck as his hands cupped her bottom through her snug riding breeches.

"I can't help it. I get hard watching you brush your teeth."

"You say the sweetest things." She laughed, kissing him on the lips before turning to the feed bin. She scooped grain into two large plastic buckets. "Grab one of these, will you?"

"You're not too shabby with the sweet talk, yourself," he said, reaching for one of the buckets.

"Hey, don't think you're out of hot water over that eggplant comment."

Thirty minutes later, the horses fed and released back into the pasture, they drove the twenty miles into the Atlanta suburb where Mia's mother, Jess, lived.

"I think they're going to make an announcement tonight," Mia said. Her mother had been dating Bill Maxwell, the chief of Atlanta Major Crimes, for almost a year. Their relationship had escalated and lately the chief spent more nights at Jessie's post-war ranch in Doraville than he did his Buckhead condo.

"You mean like an engagement announcement?" Jack said.

"Yup."

"How do you feel about that?"

"It's not like he's going to be my daddy. Mom adores him and he's crazy about her."

"Doesn't he have a daughter?"

"He does. So it looks like I get my own wicked stepsister in the bargain."

"You've met her?"

"Unfortunately, yes. She's a bitch."

"I see. And did you come to this assessment by physically slapping hands on her?"

Mia's ability to accurately read a person by touch was a gift she shared with her mother.

"I didn't have to." She gave him a crooked smile. "Even *you* could have read her feelings, Jack. But it doesn't matter. We don't have to like each other. I'm not out to steal her father."

"No, but she might think your mom is."

"Mindy is a grown woman. Married, even. With a kid."

"Doesn't matter."

"I'll take your word for it. Don't we have to stop and get wine? You know all Mom has is Blue Nun."

A look of sudden seriousness came over Jack's face as he course-corrected to the nearest liquor store on Peachtree Industrial Parkway.

*****

He would never tire of looking at her. To watch Mia laugh, pour a glass of wine, scrutinize the instructions on a microwave frozen peas package—all of it kept Jack in constantly captivated thrall. And it wasn't just the sex, although watching her was usually just a step away from imagining her shedding whatever outfit she was currently wearing.

They'd worn each other out the last two months. As exquisite as he'd imagined it in the months before—and boy had he imagined it—the reality of it was a thousand times better.

There was no doubt in his mind he was in love with her. *That* was probably true even before they'd made love. No, he was all in, full stop and without question. But where was Mia in all this? She was an eager and enthusiastic lover—ready any time he was—but how much of that was because she'd never done it before?

And how much was because it was him?

"Yo, Earth to Jack," Mia said, tapping the side of her wineglass. "The chief and I finally figured out how to open the stupid champagne; thanks a lot by the way." She turned to her mother. "Jack's an effing *sommelier*, for crap's sake. Why were we struggling with this?"

"'Cause the man's worn out," Maxwell said, his face flushed pink with his own joke. "Probably hasn't

9

had a full night's sleep since the two of you discovered how to make fire together."

Jack grinned. It did *not* do to let your mind wander with this group. The ones who weren't professional detectives had paranormal gifts that practically let them read your damn mind. His eyes went to Mia. Some, both at once.

Mia handed him a glass of champagne. "Want to make the toast?"

"Sure." He lifted his glass to the couple on the couch in front of him. "To the best home cook I know."

"That's high praise coming from Jack," Mia said to her mother. "Although slightly random given the occasion."

Jessie laughed. She had Mia's exotic dark looks, but her eyes were brown and unreadable, whereas Mia's were clear blue and easily advertised every thought she was having.

"If I may continue," Jack said, clearing his throat.

"Gosh," Mia said to her mother. "Ever been reprimanded in a toast before?"

Jessie laughed again, then looked at Maxwell. Her eyes lit up as they fell on him and Jack couldn't help thinking he wanted someone to look at him like that.

Correction. He wanted *Mia* to look at him like that.

"To an amazing woman and a man among men who, together, are the perfect match, and love's ideal."

"Ooh, that's a good one, Jack," Mia said, sipping from her glass.

"I'll never know what I did to deserve this woman saying yes to me," Maxwell said, his eyes glittering with emotion.

"We're still talking about the proposal, right?" Mia said.

"Very funny, smartass," Maxwell growled to laughter from Jack and Jessie.

"All right, Mia," Jessie said, getting up from the couch and bestowing a kiss on Maxwell's cheek. "Help me in the kitchen."

"Hey, you're not going to let her actually cook anything in there?" Jack said.

"I resemble that remark!" Mia said as Jessie pulled her toward the kitchen.

Jack sat down on the couch next to Maxwell.

"Pretty big step," he said. Jack had worked under Maxwell for nearly thirteen years during his time as a detective for the Atlanta Police Department's Major Crimes. They'd never been close but things had started to change in the last year.

"I'm the luckiest man in the world," Maxwell said, draining his glass.

"Jess's pretty lucky, too."

A moment passed when the only sounds in the house were the soft clanging of pots and pans in the kitchen and the murmur of the voices of the women they loved.

"So," Jack said. "Anything going on downtown?"

"Made an arrest today in the Internet Hussy case."

"That was fast." The newspapers had gotten playful with the city's latest scandalous murder, although Jack had to think the word "hussy" could've been updated.

A woman had been murdered in her Peachtree Corners condo—stabbed twenty-four times with a pair of scissors. The excitement from the case originated from the fact she appeared to be a dating service junkie. Evidence showed she'd contacted or dated over five hundred men in the Atlanta area in the last three years.

"Was it someone from the Internet dating service?"

"Yep. Turns out she was blackmailing him."

"Over what?"

"Kiddie porn."

"The having it or the doing it?"

"The latter." Maxwell made a face of distaste.

"What was he doing with your vic?"

"He thought she was setting him up with underage twins."

"Was she?"

"That part's unclear."

"So it was a scam?"

Maxwell set his champagne glass down. "She was a member of *Atlanta Loves* Online Dating Service, where she had a habit of trolling through likely candidates until she found someone to take the bait."

"The bait being…"

"Twin fourteen year-olds."

"I see."

"Our vic went to an ATM with our suspect and got him to hand over a thousand dollars in cash, whereupon she took him to where the girls were, secretly photographed them together then, before anything sexual happened, took the guy's money and told him if he notified the police she'd publish the photos."

"And the suspect?"

Maxwell shrugged. "A weak alibi, a few priors for underage sex, and oh yeah, we have his shoe prints all over the crime scene."

"Christmas came early for you. DNA match at the scene?"

"Not yet but we feel good."

"Means, motive and opportunity. Sounds like the holy trinity to me."

"You guys getting religious in here?" Mia came into the room carrying a steaming casserole and set it down on the dining room table.

"Something like that," Jack said. He hopped up to assist. "Oh, did I mention we got a new case?"

Mia snapped her head in his direction. "When? What is it?"

"No talking business during dinner," Jessie said firmly, setting a basket of freshly baked biscuits on the table.

Jack grinned at Mia. *Later*, he mouthed to her, meaning so much more than that.

Susan Kiernan-Lewis

2

"Tell me again why you get to carry a gun and not me?" Mia asked. She stood with her hands on her hips, watching Jack secure his Glock in his shoulder harness.

"We've been over this, Mia. You accidentally shoot inanimate objects when you carry. Inanimate objects that then cost the agency money to replace."

"*One* time that happened." Mia shrugged into her coat. It was February and bitter cold—especially at nine o'clock at night. She slapped her gloves against her thigh.

"Do we have to argue about this every time you see me strap on my piece?" Jack moved to her. "Normally you like it when I'm armed," he whispered into her ear.

She pushed him away and walked to the door. "What I do not like is being treated like a six-year-old when I am a full partner with you in this detective agency."

Jack sighed and picked up the car keys. "Mia, as I've said, I have no problem with you carrying a gun as soon as you learn how to use it. But every time I suggest we go to the range—"

"Everybody doesn't learn the same way, Jack," Mia said, her eyes flashing with annoyance. "Just because I'm not doing it your way doesn't mean that's the only way to learn."

"Practicing at a gun range is a pretty standard method," he said, tossing the keys in his hands.

"Well, so is learning by doing—in the tactical environment."

"No way. Not until I see some radical improvement in how you handle a gun."

"Why are *you* the one who has to see 'radical improvement?' That is so condescending."

"Hey, go to the range with the chief if you'd prefer. No problem."

Mia knew Maxwell was just as hardheaded as Jack when it came to wanting Mia to spend endless hours at the shooting range. When would these two by-the-book types realize that just because she approached things differently it didn't mean wrongly?

They got into the car without speaking but Mia knew she couldn't last. "I'm just a little sick of the paternalistic hand-holding, if you want to know. In general."

"Not wanting you to shoot yourself or an innocent bystander is not paternalistic," Jack said as he navigated out of the parking lot.

"Whatever," she said, refusing to look at him, concentrating instead on the scenery as it passed.

"Want to stop for coffee?"

"No, thank you. Can you fill me in on the details of the case? That is if you can trust me with that much information."

"Mia—"

"Just the basics, please, so I have some idea of what we're doing tonight."

Mia wasn't sure why she was so out of sorts. It hadn't even started with the whole stupid gun thing—although that didn't help. This case was one of the first real opportunities she and Jack had to work together and she was looking forward to showing him how much she'd improved. He was always accusing her of going off half-cocked and this was her chance to demonstrate to him she could work as a team.

"Okay, our client, Ed Patterson, owns a mid-sized wholesale operation employing thirty people. His company makes fire extinguishers."

"Where?"

"Off 85 and Lindbergh."

There was a stretch of warehouses and other wholesale facilities tucked under I-85 where it intersected Buford Highway. Most people didn't go there unless they worked at one of the factories—or unless they were into creating graffiti on any of the several pillars and cement overpass bridgeways.

"Patterson thinks an employee is stealing inventory and he needs us to confirm that."

"Doesn't he have surveillance cameras?"

"Yes, but the employee knows where they are."

"So what are you thinking? Stake out the place at night and catch him in the act?"

"Basic but effective. Sound good?" He reached over and squeezed her knee and Mia felt a twinge of guilt. *He can't help wanting to protect me all the time. It's who he is on a basic level—a guy who wants to keep everyone safe.*

Wasn't that one of the main things she loved about him?

Too bad it was also extremely damned annoying.

"Sure," she said. "Should we stop for stakeout food?" She smiled at him. "I know it's practically your most favorite part of the job."

He grinned and she felt a warm flush cascade through her chest. She loved seeing him happy. She hated being the reason when he wasn't. It was all so confusing!

"I thought we'd stop at Henri's," he said, "and grab some roast beef and horseradish sandwiches. Sound good?"

"I'm sorry for being so cranky, Jack. I'll go to the range more. You're right. That makes more sense."

He turned and smiled at her. There it was again. She just made the sun come out and shine through him like God, himself. Was it normal to have this kind of effect on someone?

"I love you, Jack," she said before she knew the words were coming out of her mouth.

The smile dropped from his face, and for one horrible moment he looked stricken. He swerved the car off the road and into a strip mall parking lot, braking abruptly before turning to her. When he did, she saw he wasn't stricken at all.

"I love you, too, Mia," he said, reaching for her hands. "I can't believe you said it. I didn't know if you —"

She laughed. "You mean, you can't believe I said it first." She unbuckled her seatbelt and launched into his arms to cover his face with kisses.

"I love you," he whispered into her hair as he held her. "I can't believe how much."

She pulled back and held his face in her hands. "Me, too." She kissed his lips, losing herself in the warmth and need in his reaction. "Don't even think about it," she whispered as he fumbled for his own seatbelt. "Jack, *no*, we are in a public parking lot with people shopping at Jiffy Mart not two doors away."

She took in a sharp intake of breath as she felt his hand slip between her legs. "I swear to God, Jack," she gasped, "if you get us arrested for public indecency..." She couldn't finish the thought. She was too busy trying to help him rip away enough clothes so she could straddle him in the driver's seat.

He pushed the seat back and eased her onto his cock, hard and ready for her. She moaned as he entered her and held him tight, her eyes barely open but seeing over his shoulder in the dusk as people came and went from the surrounding parking lot. As she moved her hips faster and faster over him, she was torn between wanting the moment to last—to hell with being safe—and wanting to hurry the feeling that promised to explode into her core.

Twenty minutes later, on their way to Henri's for their roast beef sandwiches, Mia put a hand on Jack's arm as he drove and laughed.

"What's funny?" he asked.

"I was just wondering. If that's how we celebrate our first I-love-you, what in hell would we do if we decide to get married?"

He glanced at her and then back to the road. "If?"

"Is that a proposal?" She sat straight up to give him her whole attention.

"I'm in this for the long haul, Mia. You have to know that."

A thrill of pleasure tingled through her chest. "Yeah. I think I do," she said, touching his hair where it met his collar.

"So we can afford to wait, right?"

"To see how things play out?"

"No, *not* to see how things play out. Just…take it slow. Enjoy the ride." He waggled his eyebrows at her and she laughed again.

Now, how in the world had this wonderful day started out so shitty? She honestly could not remember.

*****

Mindy Payne sat across from her five-year-old daughter watching the child concentrate on coloring a drawing. Bethany looked like her, everyone said so, which meant she looked like Mindy's grandmother. Maxwell women tended to be meek looking: washed out, pale round faces against nondescript brown hair. Mindy's mother—not a true Maxwell, of course—had broken ranks by bleaching her brown hair an aggressive shade of honey blonde.

In Mindy's opinion, it hadn't worked. And if the fact that her dad eventually divorced them and left while Cindy Maxwell was still in her prime was any evidence at all, it hadn't worked as far as *he* was concerned either.

"Careful, Bethany," Mindy said as she moved the child's juice cup out of reach. "We don't want to make a mess in Mommy's clean kitchen."

The child didn't look up. Mindy frowned. She took after Tad in that way. Her husband could walk through a room and pieces of clothing, mail and other detritus would just naturally fall off him—leaving Mindy to tidy up in his wake.

"It can't spill," the child said, squinting at her drawing.

"What?"

"The juice. It has a lid on it."

"Let's just be careful, all right?" Was that lip? Was she being disrespectful? God, if so she was starting early. Mindy's own mother loved to tell stories of what a monster Mindy had been growing up. If Mindy remembered correctly, and of course she did, her father said it showed she had backbone.

A million years ago.

"Mommy has to make a phone call," Mindy said as she stood, her smartphone in hand. Honestly, it was never out of hand. Tad claimed she slept with it under her pillow at night. She just needed to know things. The mystery to her was why he wasn't that way too.

She stepped out of the kitchen and walked to the dining room. She'd positioned the kitchen table, where Bethany worked, at an angle such that Mindy could see it—and Bethany—from nearly twenty feet away. Far enough away to not be heard on personal phone calls, close enough to guard against the child's natural propensity to destroy her environment.

At first Mindy had debated using a burner phone for this call, but decided it defeated the whole purpose if the bitch didn't know who she was.

"Hello?" It always amazed Mindy to hear the woman's voice. She'd only met her once and had been startled then too. Jess Kazmaroff had a voice like silk, smooth and undulating. No wonder her father was seduced by her.

"Yes, hello, Jess, this is Mindy Payne. I hope I didn't catch you at a bad time?"

"Not at all. I'm glad to hear from you. I imagine your father told you our news?"

"Yes, and frankly, that's why I'm calling. I need to ask you not to do this. Please."

"I'm sorry?"

"My parents were—are—incredibly close to a reconciliation. I don't suppose my father mentioned that to you?"

The woman didn't respond but Mindy heard the quick intake of breath on the line.

"Well, anyway," Mindy said. "He has problems communicating, trust me, and I wanted to make sure you knew them before you got…too much further along. I don't want anyone else to get hurt by my father."

"I see."

"Well, I really hope you do, and I also hope I don't have to call again. Trust me, this isn't pleasant for me either. Can you tell me you understand what I'm saying?"

"Oh, I think I can tell you that, dear."

"Awesome." Mindy hung up and felt a surge of relief rush. That wasn't so bad. True, her father would probably hear from the woman and have to endure the tears and hysteria Jess had been too prideful to show Mindy. But still…it had to be done. One thing Mindy knew, her father was about as spineless when it came to saying the things that needed to be said as a jelly fish.

Bethany turned her head to look at Mindy and then looked back to her drawing. Mindy's rush of pleasure left in the time it took to snap a crayon in two.

What the hell was that child up to?

*****

So far, the best part of the night—except for the strip mall sex—was the roast beef. Jack eased a crick out of his neck and rubbed his eyes. Mia had gone looking for a restroom at the gas station on the corner—a good half-mile back—and while she had her cellphone on her, he still didn't love the idea of her walking back alone in the dark.

Love. He grinned and his aching neck stopped hurting for as long as he remembered the moment when she'd blurted out *I love you.* The look on her face half convinced him she hadn't meant to say it. Hell, maybe she hadn't. It didn't matter now. That was one episode of wild parking lot sex and several references to *maybe we'll get married* ago. God, he had it bad. And it felt great.

Jack twisted in his seat to see if Mia was visible yet on her way back. The whole point of the stakeout was not to be seen. He hoped she remembered that. A light flickered from the plain cinder block building in front of him, catching his eye. He saw a door closing—the interior light obviously what he'd seen for a flash.

Jack's body tensed and all his senses sharpened. A figure was walking close to the side of the building— clearly someone who knew where the surveillance cameras were positioned. He had a large box in his hands.

Show time! Jack slipped out of the car and pressed the door shut quietly before dropping into a crouch.

Where the hell was Mia? He felt for the camera in his jacket pocket. He didn't have to intercept the guy. Just needed to photograph his guilty-ass face as he tried to load the box into his trunk before then confirming the box's contents. Jack had a rough schematic of the office building showing two parking lots, one feeding into the other, all of it enclosed in an unlocked eight-foot chain link fence. He and Mia had parked in the lot closest to the building but the guy was hurrying into the smaller one, probably where he'd parked his car.

Jack stayed low and crept up behind one of the few other parked cars in the lot. The figure was fishing in his jacket now for his car keys. Jack needed to stop him before he reached his car. He stood up and trotted straight for him.

The guy saw him and immediately dropped the box. Jack heard the telltale clang of metal hitting the pavement.

"Yo, dude," Jack said. "Got a light?" He pulled out his camera. He'd be close enough in another five seconds to get the guy's face in frame. Suddenly the guy turned and bolted for the chain link fence beyond the office building. There was always a chance these things went down the hard way and this looked to be one of those times. Jamming the camera back in his pocket, Jack took off after him.

The guy had a twenty-foot head start. Jack saw him hit the fence and start to climb over it and Jack stopped running. What was the point? Even without a picture he could identify him. All Jack had to do was grab the stolen box and call the cops.

"Stop or I'll shoot!"

Mia's words rang out in the cold night air like something out of Jack's worst nightmare.

3

Mia stood at the corner of the warehouse, her arms shaking as she held her hairbrush pointed at the man. When she watched him clamber over the fence with Jack right behind, she had just enough time to wrench the brush from her purse and step into the beam of the one security light.

She felt a flush of heat as she watched the man turn slowly to face her. His eyes glanced down at the brush in her hands. By then the sounds of Jack coming over the top of the fence filled the air between them. The look on the man's face—white with fury and frustration—triggered her next move. She flung the brush at him and turned to run, a scream coming out of her before she could stop it.

The impact as the man hit her from behind punched the air out of her. She felt the night world swirling about her as he whipped her around. Her legs gave out, but he held her up, his face close to hers, his breath labored and smelling of onions and fish.

The icy prick of a knife blade brought her back to the world and she struggled to stand on her own.

"Get the fuck back in your car or I kill her," he snarled into Mia's hair. She realized he wasn't speaking to her.

"Let her go."

"You're trespassing. People get hurt when they trespass." The man shook Mia, his supporting hand snaking up her back to hold her securely by the hair. He tugged her head back, exposing her throat more. The knife pinched into her skin. She felt his fear where he touched her, sliding over like a writhing cottonmouth.

"Don't make it worse," Jack said. He sounded closer now. "Nobody gets the needle for grand theft."

Mia's squeezed her eyes shut. Her captor's panting was all she could hear. Suddenly he released his grip on her hair. She brought her chin down a fraction when she felt herself being pushed away. The ground flew up to smash her in the face.

The audio in her world muted as she huddled on the ground, waiting for the grassy field to stop spinning long enough to look around. It felt like hours that she lay there, staring at the grass, when she started to hear noises again.

Terrible noises.

The sounds of fists pummeling flesh, over and over again. She lifted her head and twisted in the direction of the noises and saw the two of them on the ground, Jack on top, punching, hitting. Mia shook her head, but the motion caused a roiling in her gut and she vomited down the front of her jacket.

"Jack," she said weakly. "Don't…kill him."

*****

As Jess turned on the porch light she reminded herself the important thing was that Mia was safe. And Jack, too, of course. She still held the cell phone in her hand following Bill's hurried call to her. *Everybody safe. That's all the matters.*

She went back to the couch and tucked her feet under her, setting the cell phone down and picking up the remote control. Mia's little dog, Daisy, curled up next to her and Jess put a hand on her, feeling the warmth like a soothing balm. It has been such a pleasant night before the phone call from Jack came. Bill had his jacket on and was walking out the door before he even heard all the details.

Jess smiled. That was so like him. Her smile wavered and then dropped. She turned off the television. It wasn't going to be possible to be distracted by it tonight. The edge that had slipped into the evening—the first time Jess ever remembered feeling it between them—was subtle and pervasive, and sharp as a scalpel.

Was Mindy correct in her assessment that her father was obtuse when it came to communication? Jess had never seen it before, but tonight was a startling revelation in that way. How could anyone spend two hours over dinner and not realize something was wrong?

Did he really not know? He wasn't an intuitive, that was true, but she'd never thought him insensate.

Mindy was, of course, expecting Jess to share the phone conversation with her father. For that reason, if no other, Jess hesitated. *If I don't talk about it, did it happen? If I don't tell Bill, he doesn't have to confront Mindy, and if she's having second thoughts about making the call, perhaps we don't have to start our relationship off in damage control.*

Isn't it best when someone puts a foot wrong to avert one's eyes and pretend it didn't happen? Wouldn't Mindy thank her for that going forward? She was sure it was best not to tell Bill. He looked so happy tonight. So complete. Which brought up the bigger question once more…

Why didn't he know there was something off tonight?

*****

Now Mia knew what people meant when they said a scene looked surreal. *Here's how an everyday picture of a simple field next to a parking lot can look like something out of an episode of The Twilight Zone—sinister and full of evil.*

She sat with a blanket around her shoulders on the steps of an ambulance, a bottle of water in her hands. The police had marked off the crime scene and carted away the guy's knife in a little plastic baggie—as well as Jack's gun, although he never drew it.

The assailant was carted away too

In a coroner's wagon.

Every time she relived the moment of watching Jack step away from the guy's body, she started to shake. He'd come to her to check that she was unharmed, and then he called the cops. They sat together in silence, the body in front of them, and waited.

How did this happen? How did things go so wrong?

Now she watched Jack in the distance talking to two detectives. He wasn't in handcuffs. Yet. Another car drove up and snapped its headlights off. Mia recognized the SUV and the man climbing out of it. She was glad he'd come alone. Her mother didn't need to be here.

Maxwell walked over to where the detectives and Jack were talking.

Good. The chief will get things sorted out.

Won't he?

Mia tried to push the image out of her mind of Jack straddling the man. It was her fault. If she hadn't tried to do an impromptu survey of the area, she wouldn't have bumped into the perp after he'd climbed the fence.

Why couldn't she just have come straight back to the car?

Jack was probably asking himself the same thing.

Maxwell turned and walked toward her. That didn't seem like a good sign. Mia peered over his shoulder and, sure enough, Jack was getting into the back of a police cruiser. Mia jumped up, the blanket falling from her shoulders.

"Chief! Where are they taking him? Are you serious? Is he under arrest?"

Maxwell held out his hands as he walked up to her, wanting to calm her before reaching her.

"They just need to finish asking their questions downtown," he said.

"Downtown? You mean before they book him? Chief, you can't let them do this."

"Mia, stop it," Maxwell said sternly. He was wearing jeans and a heavy cotton pullover. The call had caught him in the middle of a homey evening snuggling on the couch with her mother. A needle of guilt pierced her chest.

"They'll be wanting to question you, too."

"Me, why? I didn't see anything!"

"Mia, a man died here tonight. You're a witness."

"Chief, this is Jack. Whatever he said happened is what happened. What is he saying happened?"

"That the man died as he was 'questioning' him."

Mia sucked in a short breath. That almost sounded like a confession.

"What happened here tonight, Mia?" Maxwell handed the blanket to one of the EMTs, who were packing up to leave. He put his arm around Mia to lead her back to his car.

The cruiser with Jack in it backed up and drove away.

"We…we were watching for the guy—"

"What guy?"

"An employee of our client. He thought he was stealing stuff."

Maxwell nodded. "They recovered a box of new fire extinguishers out front. Go on."

"I had to go to the bathroom so I went to use the one at the Jiffy Mart about a half mile down the road."

"Alone?"

"Well, *someone* had to stay to see if our guy was going to show tonight."

Maxwell opened the car door and Mia slipped in. She supposed Jack's car would be towed. Her stomach wrenched when she thought back to the early evening when she and Jack had made such hurried, mad, urgent love in that car.

Just a few hours ago.

The chief started the car. "And so you came back to the car and found Jack gone?"

This was the part where she got to confess it was all her fault. Only it wasn't going to change the outcome or make Jack any less guilty. It was just going to show how, once again, she had screwed up and made someone else pay the price.

A heavy exhaustion crept over her. It must be past one in the morning. Maxwell cranked up the heat in the car and she could feel his attempt to rein in his impatience as he waited for her to answer.

"I thought I'd do a quick reconnaissance of the surrounding area on foot," she said quietly.

"Go on."

"When I approached the far side of the cement building I heard the fence clanging like someone was on it, and when I came around the side of the building I saw a guy jumping off it—Jack on the other side. He'd obviously been chasing him."

Maxwell still didn't speak but his finger tapped the steering wheel.

"It was my fault, Chief," Mia said, her voice low.

"What did you do?"

She took in a long breath. "I pretended like I had a gun and told him to stop. Stupid. I didn't think. I don't know what made me say it. He...he grabbed me and he had a knife."

"He held you at knifepoint," Maxwell said, his fingers tightening around the steering wheel. Clearly, he'd already heard this part from Jack.

Mia nodded. "And then Jack climbed over the fence and was talking to him, telling him to put down the knife."

"And then?" Maxwell's voice was tight.

"The rest is hazy. I somehow got shoved away and I…guess I kind of blacked out."

There was a brief pause. "Are you going to tell me you didn't see what happened?"

"I *didn't* see what happened." Mia looked at him. "What do the cops think happened? Do they think Jack killed him with his bare hands?"

"Jack was armed."

"But he didn't pull his gun."

"I thought you didn't see any of it."

Mia looked away. "He was just trying to protect me," she said, her eyes filling with tears. How could this have happened? If she'd just come back to the car like she was supposed to! If she hadn't tried to grandstand or be a super-detective, Jack wouldn't be in the back of a cop car right this minute.

"I know," Maxwell said. They didn't speak the rest of the drive back to Jessie's house.

*****

Jack stayed downtown the rest of that night. Maxwell wouldn't allow Mia to go to him and so she waited in her mother's house, drinking decaf until she finally fell asleep on the living room sofa. When she awoke, Maxwell and Jessie were having coffee in the kitchen.

Mia staggered into the room, hair tousled, her mascara smeared and glued to her cheeks.

"Did they book him?" she blurted.

Maxwell sighed and put his mug of coffee down while Jessie hopped up to get a cup for Mia. He looked immaculately dressed, as if he'd had a good night's sleep and hours to shave, shower, press a knife-edge on his slacks and de-lint his jacket. The truth was, he had still been up when Mia fell asleep.

"They did," Maxwell said. "Manslaughter. I'm going now to post bail."

Mia sat down hard on one of the kitchen chairs. "Manslaughter," she murmured. "The guy was trying to hurt me. He had a knife. Jack was unarmed."

"He wasn't," Maxwell said.

"But he didn't pull his gun," Mia said, jumping up. "Did the guy die of a gunshot wound? What the hell does it matter if Jack had a gun if he didn't use it?"

"She has a point, dearest," Jessie said to Maxwell as she slid the mug of hot coffee across the table to Mia.

"Unfortunately, it's an irrelevant one," Maxwell said.

"Well, what did the Medical Examiner say the guy died of?" Mia asked.

"We don't have his full report yet."

"I don't give a shit about how many enzymes he had in his stomach! Give me the fucking CliffsNotes version. How did he die?"

"Mia, please. Language," Jessie said, frowning.

"He bled to death," Maxwell said, standing and straightening his shirt cuffs. "From a ruptured spleen, the result of blunt force trauma."

Mia shook her head. *This was unbelievable. Jack ruptured the guy's spleen?*

"Nothing else?" she asked weakly. "Was there no other possible reason he could have died?"

"The ME said he bled out and died within minutes."

Mia stood. "Give me five minutes to get dressed."

"I will," Maxwell said, "but you're not coming downtown with me. I'll drop you off in Atlantic Station."

Before she could protest, he put up a hand. "Last word on the subject."

"No time for breakfast?" Jessie asked.

"I'm sure Jack will appreciate it if, just this once, we skip it," Maxwell said, leaning over to kiss her.

After Maxwell dropped her off at her condo, Mia spent the rest of the morning cleaning house. It was already tidy but she needed to keep busy until Maxwell brought Jack home.

It was my fault. I know that's what Jack is thinking and he's right.

Vowing to confess responsibility the moment he stepped across the threshold, Mia wiped down the inside of the refrigerator, mopped the kitchen floor and started a load of laundry. Jack liked to kid her about how non-domestic she was, so Mia hoped he would see these out-of-character efforts as testimony to how serious she took her responsibility in last night's events.

Because she was in the laundry room with her head in the dryer, she didn't hear them come in. Jack's voice came down the hall ahead of him. "I'm not doing a fucking plea. That's the end of it." Mia dropped the laundry basket and ran to the living room. Jack was on the phone and didn't look at her when she entered the room. Maxwell stood staring out the living room window.

"Because I'm innocent, how about that?" Jack said into the phone. "Does that work for you?" He hung up and turned to Mia. He gave her a tired smile and opened his arms. She slipped into them and held him tight.

"Oh, Jack, I'm so sorry."

"It's okay," he said, kissing her hair.

"If it wasn't for me…" She pulled back to see his eyes. "If I had just come back to the car."

"Woulda shoulda coulda," Maxwell said, as he turned from the window. "I'm heading back. You need anything else?"

Jack disengaged himself from Mia and shook hands with Maxwell.

"Thanks, Chief," he said. "I owe you one."

"All right then," Maxwell said. "Take care of our girl here and keep me apprised of your case."

After he left, Mia turned to Jack.

"What did they say? What happens next? Do you… do you still have your gun?"

He shook his head and ran a hand over his eyes. It occurred to Mia he probably didn't sleep last night.

"No, nor my PI license either. At least temporarily."

"Who were you talking to when you came in?"

"My lawyer."

"That was fast. You were arguing. He wants you to plead guilty? Why did they charge you?"

"Basically, they say I used undue force for the situation."

"They know the guy had a knife to my throat?"

"They do. They believe, since I disarmed him, that he should still be alive."

"Why…do you know what happened?"

"What do you mean?"

"Do you know…why he isn't? I didn't see any of it, Jack. I don't know what happened."

Jack let out a long sigh and shrugged. "Do you mind if I don't do this again right now? That is literally all I've talked about for nine hours."

"No, of course not. Why don't you go take a shower while I make sandwiches?"

"Sounds good." He stood up slowly and groaned.

"Want some company?"

He smiled but shook his head. "Maybe next time."

Mia watched him leave the room, his shoulders slumped. She turned back to the kitchen, a feeling of foreboding vibrating up her spine.

He had never passed up the opportunity to get naked with her before.

4

The next morning, Mia was up before Jack. It was a Saturday, which meant he had a dinner party he was cooking for that night, and yet he was still in bed. Last night, for the first time in two months, Mia was tempted to sleep in her own bedroom to give him the time to really rest. In the end, she decided that wasn't a good habit to get into and just made sure she didn't disturb him while he slept.

Now, as she set down a tray full of buttered toast and two mugs of coffee on the dresser, she saw he was awake.

"Hey," she said. "You okay?"

He blinked his eyes and rubbed his face before answering. "Just tired."

"Don't you have a dinner you're private cheffing tonight?"

"I do." He twisted around to pick up his cell phone and squinted at the time. "Shit. It's late."

"You needed the sleep."

Jack reached for his coffee and smiled wanly at her.

"It's going to be okay, Mia."

"I know. I just wish it was over. Can you tell me a little bit about it now?"

He sighed and returned his mug to the side table. For a minute, Mia thought he was about to turn over and go back to sleep.

"I was charged with voluntary manslaughter."

"Is that worse than plain old manslaughter?"

"Yeah, it means I meant to kill him. As opposed to…I didn't mean to."

"Are there cameras that caught it?" Mia dropped her voice and looked away.

Manslaughter. He had been protecting her and he went too far.

"Yeah. Look at me, Mia."

Mia snapped her head up to face him.

"I didn't kill him," he said.

She nodded but didn't speak.

"I didn't, Mia."

"Well, not on purpose…" she said softly, looking away.

"Is that what you think? That I lost control and killed him?" His voice was cold, and when she brought her eyes to meet his they were unreadable.

"I think, sometimes, you have a tendency to… overreact to things."

"Holy shit. I can't believe I'm hearing what I'm hearing." He flung the covers back and climbed out of bed, making Mia jump back. "Guess it's a good thing I don't need you as a character witness."

"Jack, don't be like this. Just tell me what happened. If the ME is wrong and the cops are wrong and the security camera and my own eyes are all wrong —"

"I thought you didn't see anything."

"I saw enough."

"What exactly?" He stood in front of her, his hands on his hips, naked yet powerful.

"I saw you straddling the guy and…hitting him."

"You can't have."

"I saw what I saw, Jack. Doesn't mean I'm not on your side."

"Great. You think I did it but you'll wait for me to get out of prison. Swell."

"Well, you *did* do it."

"I was hoping you'd believe in me, Mia."

"Facts have nothing to do with belief! I *believe* in you no matter what you've done."

He turned and walked into the bathroom, closing the door firmly behind him. After a moment, Mia heard the shower go on. Should she not have told him the truth? She picked up the tray with the uneaten toast, her arms feeling heavy with sadness and indecision.

There was so much white in the bridal shop, Mia felt like she was walking through a bank of clouds. Wedding dresses hung in walls of thick ivory curtains of lace and taffeta, billowing out on every wall of the shop. She sat next to Ned in a plush chair waiting for Jess to emerge from the dressing room.

"Jack's speaking to me," Mia said, "but he's just not saying anything worth hearing."

"I'm not surprised," Ned said, sipping coffee from a tall travel mug. "Way to withdraw support."

"Ned, I saw what I saw. Jack on top of the guy slugging the crap out of him."

"And the security cameras confirm that?"

"Yes and no. You can see the guy grab me with the knife to my throat and you can see Jack step in and karate chop him to knock the knife away, but we all fall out of view then."

"So is it just your word against Jack's?"

"No. I gave my statement that I didn't see anything. I won't have to testify against him."

"How bad is it?"

"Bad. Although Jack's not in a sharing place right now, I've overheard a few things in his conversation with his lawyer."

"So if they convict him will he do serious time? He's an ex-cop for crap's sake."

"Him being a cop is the reason he's out on bail. That and whatever pull Maxwell has."

"How much was it?"

"I have no idea. The chief handled it. It just hurts that Jack thinks I don't support him."

"Well, you kind of don't, Mia." Ned shrugged. "The guy says he didn't kill the dude and you say he did."

"I saw what I *saw*," Mia muttered, but felt tears prick at her eyes. She wiped at them quickly as her mother came into the presentation room wearing a long tea-colored gown, the train following regally behind.

"Wow, Mrs. K," Ned said, clapping his hands together. "That's stunning."

Jessie pivoted in front of the three-way mirror. Beadwork studded down the bustle to the hem. The A-line silhouette in the gown nipped her waist and then fell into a train of chiffon.

"It is pretty, isn't it?"

"Mom, you look like a princess in that one." Mia said, jumping up to get a better look.

"Well," Jessie said, eyeing her reflection critically and then breaking into a smile. "I *am* marrying my prince after all."

"Aw, Mrs. K," Ned said. "That is so sweet."

"So I'm going to get this one," Jessie said with a nod.

"But, Mom, it's literally the first one you tried on." Mia walked around her mother. She had to admit this one would be hard to top.

"You know when you've found the right one," Jessie said pointedly to Mia. "Ned, dear, would you be an angel and tell Katie that I need assistance in the fitting room?"

As Ned left, Jessie turned to Mia and took both her hands.

"In case things get so hectic that I don't get a chance to tell you, Mia," Jessie said, "marrying Bill takes nothing away from how much I loved your father."

"I know that, Mom."

"But having said that, this day—my wedding day—is one of the most important of my life. Do you understand?"

"I think so. I won't wear leather, arrive late or get any noticeable piercings or tats before then."

Jessie kissed her daughter on the cheek. "After Bill, you are the most important person in my life, dear girl," she said, her eyes filling, "and I need you to make sure that nothing, and I mean nothing, prevents you from being there—at my side—when I take Bill as my husband."

"Sure, Mom. Of course." A wave of uneasiness passed through Mia. Her mother's hand on her tingled with anticipation, love and…worry. They weren't emotions Mia was unfamiliar with coming from her mother—but at the intensity she was feeling them now, yes, this was different.

"I know the chief makes you happy, Mom," Mia said. "I love him, too."

Jessie squeezed Mia's hand just as the saleswoman bustled toward them two steps ahead of Ned. When she and Jessie disappeared into the dressing room, Ned nudged Mia.

"So what'd your mom want to speak to you alone about? Did you give her some hints for the wedding night? Probably been awhile."

"She wanted to make sure I'd be there. Kind of hurt my feelings a little. I mean, is she really worried I won't make it?"

"Come on, Mia, this is you we're talking about. Duh."

"I'd die rather than miss her wedding."

"Well, *then* you'd miss it for sure, so whatever your mama told you to do, just do it, girl."

When Mia got back to the condo—with little Daisy in tow—Jack was in the kitchen packing for his dinner party. Normally, Mia enjoyed watching him wrap up his favorite knives, pans and spices in his wire utility cart. He wore a starched white chef's uniform. She used to tease him about getting a toque to finish the look. He didn't look to be in the mood for teasing at the moment.

"What's on the menu tonight?" she asked, as she dropped her car keys in the bowl by the door. Daisy ran to Jack and he squatted down to greet her.

"I'm glad you brought this one back to the condo," he said, not looking at Mia. "She's a good little watchdog, aren't you, Daisy?"

Mia waited patiently for his greeting of the dog to wind down. "Should I be jealous?"

He stood and gave Mia a kiss on the cheek.

"Wow. So not jealous," Mia said, "but definitely worried."

"I'm just in a hurry," Jack said.

"I can count the orgasms on both hands the last time you were 'in a hurry,'" Mia said, crossing her arms.

"You do know I've been arrested for killing a man, right?" he said, returning to his cart. "So I might be a little distracted these days"

"Have you talked to your lawyer today?"

"No news."

"When's the preliminary hearing set for?"

"Mia, I'm late. Let's pick this up later."

"I'll wait up."

"No, don't. I'll be after two."

"I don't mind."

"Mia, no. We'll talk in the morning."

She followed him to the front door. "I got a call about a possible new case," she said. "A gay couple working in midtown. One of them thinks the other's cheating on him."

"You handle it."

"Alone?"

"Mia, what part of *I lost my license* is confusing to you?" Jack raised his voice. "If you want to take a case, you'll need to handle it without me. I'm sorry. I'm just really late now." He leaned in and gave her a quick kiss on the cheek and was gone.

Daisy ran to the door after Mia shut it and looked up at her.

"We'll get through it," Mia said to the dog before turning back to the kitchen. Jack had prepared her dinner, foiled the top and scribbled baking instructions on a post-it note attached to it.

Even mad and disgusted, he still takes care of me.

She set the oven temperature, found a cookie sheet and peeked under the foil. Chicken something. Didn't matter. Jack knew what she liked. Her cell phone rang and she dug it out from her purse perched on one of the dining room chairs. The screen said *Bentley and Jamison*, a law office in town Jack and Mia had worked with before.

"Mia Kazmaroff," she answered crisply.

"Oh, good, Ms. Kazmaroff. My name is George Peterson. I'm an attorney with Bentley and Jamison law firm. I have a case for you that I hope you'll be interested in taking."

Mia sat down at the kitchen counter and pulled a notepad out of a drawer and fumbled for a pen.

"Absolutely, Mr. Peterson," she said. "Can you give me some information?"

"Have you heard of the Internet Hussy case? It's been in the news quite a bit."

Mia hesitated. The murder of an attractive young woman who used a local dating service to find her victims had been in the papers fairly steadily all month. "I have," she said, tapping her pen against the paper. "Didn't the cops solve that case?"

"Well, it depends on your perspective. I am the defense attorney for the man they believe killed Victoria Baskerville."

Before Peterson finished his words Mia felt her mouth dry as excitement began to well up inside her. This was a very big case. Bentley and Jamison didn't do public defense work.

"You need us to find out who else might have killed Ms. Baskerville," Mia said, forcing herself to sound professional.

"Can you meet to discuss the details of the case before you decide?"

"I'm free any time this week," Mia said, tossing the pen down.

"I'll meet you at your offices tomorrow morning at eight o'clock," he said.

After Mia hung up, she glanced at the kitchen wall clock and then called Maxwell.

"Just on my way to your mother's," he answered. "What's up?"

"I got a new case. One I think you know a few things about. I was wondering if you could give me a quick briefing before I meet my client."

"Who is it?"

"George Peterson with Bentley and Jamison. He's defending your prime suspect in the Victoria Baskerville case."

"I know who he is. What do you want to know? Keep in mind that if you take the case, we'll be on opposite teams and I won't be sharing anything with you."

"Can you tell me the facts of the case that aren't in dispute?"

Maxwell sighed. Mia could hear traffic on his end and wondered if she hadn't gotten very lucky catching him in rush hour.

"Thirty-two-year-old vic stabbed to death in her apartment," he said. "She was running a scam on men she trolled for on a local online dating service called *Atlanta Loves*."

"What was the scam?"

"She promised her marks sex with underage twins, emptied out their ATMs, then blackmailed them with covert photos to keep them from coming after her."

"Ouch. And everybody's surprised she ended up stabbed to death?"

"Twenty-four times."

"So my client's client…he's a pedophile?"

"Well, that would be a logical conclusion to draw considering what he was doing with Ms. Baskerville."

"Yeah, I'm not thinking I want to help a child molester beat the rap."

"Glad to hear it."

"Okay. Well, thanks, Chief. Hurrying home to the little woman?"

"Goodbye, Mia."

Mia hung up. She debated calling Peterson back to cancel, but decided she'd at least hear him out. His client must have money for them to be defending him on this. *Even if he didn't kill Baskerville, he's still a disgusting perv who deserves to go to prison.* She hopped up to slide her dinner into the hot oven then take a quick shower before supper. The little dog trotted at her heels.

*****

The next morning, Jack stood in the kitchen watching the espresso maker heat up.

"How desperate do you have to be to take this case?" he said.

"I didn't say we were taking the case." Mia was seated at the kitchen counter. "I'm just talking to the guy today."

"Why are you even talking to him? And it's not 'we,' remember."

"Yeah, I get it, Jack. You're out for the game."

"I mean, what is it about a sexual deviant that brings out your nurturing side?" He turned to her. "Sorry."

He didn't want to snipe with her. Hadn't he spent all last night during the prep for the dinner party telling himself he wasn't going to take it out on her any more?

"Can't we clear the air about what's going on with you?" Mia asked.

He poured two cups of espresso and slid one in front of her. He took in a long breath and let it out. "The guy seemed to stop breathing as soon as I threw him down," he said. "What you saw was me trying to get his heart going again."

"But the ME said he died from a busted spleen." Her face was creased in a frown. He could tell she wanted to believe him. "His spleen didn't just self-destruct. And Jack, you were so mad."

"I don't know what to tell you, Mia."

Mia got up and went to him. She put a hand on his arm. "I'm on your side, Jack."

A part of him wanted to pull her into his arms but he felt her distance—even if she was standing right next to him. He didn't move.

"Daisy hasn't been out yet," she said, turning away.

Jack stood in the kitchen for a moment, still smelling the light wisp of perfume she left behind, and cursed.

*****

Downstairs at the front door of the offices of Burton & Kazmaroff Detective Agency—located on the first floor under her condo—Mia noticed a man standing by a black Mercedes Benz. He was looking at his cellphone but jerked his head up when she arrived.

"Ms. Kazmaroff?" he said.

"You're early," Mia said, fumbling for the keys to the office door.

George Peterson approached her. He was blond, average height, good-looking.

"If I may make a suggestion?" he said. "To save time?" He stepped back and gestured to his car. "Allow me to fill you in on the way to breakfast. If you're interested, we can go straight to where he's being held and you can interview him. If not..." He shrugged.

Mia hesitated and then decided, *why not?* She climbed into the Mercedes, nearly sliding off the slick, lush leather seating and onto the floor.

"My client's name is Josh Cook," Peterson said, backing out of the parking lot and pointing the car toward Midtown. "He was one of twenty men Ms. Baskerville scammed out of money by masquerading as a sex procurer."

"Wow. You make it sound so defensible," Mia said. "Your client admitted he contacted Victoria Baskerville in order to have sex with two underage girls, right?"

Peterson glanced at her and frowned.

"The girls were not, after all, underage, Ms. Kazmaroff."

"I see. He just thought they were. Does he have any priors?"

Peterson nodded. "He was arrested in 2010 for stalking his fourteen-year-old neighbor. Charges were dropped."

"Is he wealthy?"

"Does it matter?"

"Might explain why a lowlife like him can afford one of the best law firms in Atlanta."

"His family has money, yes," Peterson said. "But we wouldn't have taken the case for that reason alone."

"His winning personality?"

"No, he's not very nice. If you meet him, that will be clear enough."

"Then why?"

"We believe he's innocent, Ms. Kazmaroff. We need you to uncover the proof to support that."

Mia gnawed on a cuticle and glanced out the window.

"You wouldn't want the wrong person to pay for this crime, would you, Ms. Kazmaroff? Even if they repulsed you?"

"You can skip the breakfast stop," Mia said, without looking at him. "And you can skip the visit to the jail. I've heard enough."

"May I ask to what end?"

"I don't know. I just know meeting him will not help me look at this dispassionately."

Especially if I touch him. I'll probably want to drop the noose on him with my own hands.

"Fair enough."

They drove back to Atlantic Station in silence. Peterson pulled back into a parking spot and handed Mia a file folder.

"I need you to at least have all the facts before you make up your mind," he said. "Included there are several copies of pages from Victoria's diary."

Mia got out of the car with the folder.

"I'll await your call," he said, before driving off.

An hour later, Mia sat in her car, a cold Starbucks in her drink holder, the contents of the file folder spread across her front seat. She had to hand it to Peterson. He didn't sugarcoat who his client was.

Cook was a degenerate sex offender kept out of the prisons and off the streets by the fact his family had money. Mia had to stop herself from wanting to be the caped crusader who finally stopped all that. But Peterson had been right about that, too. Cook's disgusting personality and other crimes were not the point of today's meeting.

The question was: *Did he murder Victoria Baskerville?*

Mia looked up from the sheaf of scattered pages and photos. The case against Cook was weak. Which didn't mean he wouldn't go down for it. What was it Maxwell always said? Most police departments didn't have the resources to chase down every case the way it should be.

Murders went unsolved because of budgetary cuts and lack of personnel.

Mia started her car and drove down Peachtree Road until she came to the block-long building called the Alhambra Condominiums—an ochre monster of Moroccan style and Old World charm. The building, dating back to the twenties, sat on Peachtree Road, its spacious stone balconies facing the famous street. She pulled into the back parking lot and got out.

It surprised her that Victoria would choose the Alhambra to live in. It definitely had more charm than glitz, but the location was one of the best in the city— right in the heart of Buckhead and walking distance to shopping and restaurants.

Mia stood on the sidewalk in front of the building. Victoria's balcony was the second from the sweeping entrance. Even on the first floor, it hung too high off the ground to make access from the outside plausible. A stained glass window panel hung in the bedroom window. A flutter of yellow police tape from inside the condo caught Mia's eye, explaining why the place didn't have a *For Sale* sign in the window yet. She took a step back, mindful of the steady stream of traffic behind her.

As a home base, it was a little too bohemian for the picture of Victoria Baskerville painted by the media. It just didn't seem like the headquarters for a scam artist and budding pimp. *Only, she wasn't a pimp.* Promising underage girls was a part of her scam but the file indicated she never delivered. She'd walk with the marks to an ATM, empty it, then lead them to where the girls were—often right here at the Alhambra—where Victoria would covertly photograph the foreplay. The pictures in the file showed two girls in bras and panties frolicking with the suspect, Joshua Cook.

Mia's stomach tightened at the memory of the photos. The guy looked sleazy. He watched the girls with an indecent hunger in his eyes.

Then Victoria would shoo the girls away, present the patsy with her photo montage and tell him to forget her name and address unless he wanted the photos to show up on Facebook, Linked In, and the entire email address book of his cell phone.

Mia knew now why the attorney included the pages from Victoria's diary in the file. Mia only skimmed them but they succeeded in doing the one thing all the newspaper headlines couldn't. They humanized her.

Her diary pages turned the *Internet Hussy* into a young woman looking forward to Fridays with friends and planning on catching Nordstrom's latest shoe sale.

Mia wiped her hands on her jeans, surprised to discover they were damp.

Victoria lived at the Alhambra for five years. Mia envisioned her watching the Peachtree Road Race from her balcony. She must have walked across the street to the Barnes and Noble bookstore hundreds of times in five years. Two blocks down was the famous Raj Indian restaurant—a little hole-in-the-wall bistro serving the best Indian food this side of Delhi. Victoria for sure drank beers and ate pizza at the Mystic in Garden Hills, not a quarter of a mile from the Alhambra.

Only now, of course, she did none of those.

Mia walked back to her car. The temperature had dropped since she set out this morning and she noticed a low grey cloud cover hovering overhead. She should have worn her coat.

Jack was right, of course. The last thing Mia wanted to do was help a sexual deviant get off the hook—even if that hook wasn't one he baited.

What difference does it make if the little slime ball goes down for a murder he didn't commit? Isn't that karma?

But Mia knew what the difference was. Because, in the end, the case was not about saving Cook, the pedophile. She turned and looked back at the Alhambra, the sun filtering through the tall oaks that framed it.

It was about finding justice for Victoria.

5

Would I rather he just went through the motions? Mia stepped out of the shower and saw Jack was up and, if the noises coming from the kitchen meant anything, already whipping up breakfast.

Last night had been strained. He was exhausted and went to bed early—unusual for him. Mia stayed up an hour longer to flip through cable shows she had no interest in watching in order to give him plenty of time to fall asleep. Should she have reached for him in the night? Would a midnight coupling have assuaged what two nights of tension and forced civility had created?

Or would that have just made it worse?

Mia pulled on her jeans and a long sleeve T-shirt. *How can we be at this stage so soon? The stage where something's wrong and instead of talking about it we just avoid each other?* She grimaced in her bedroom mirror. She kept her hair long so she could just pull it back and not deal with it. Today it looked like she needed to deal with it.

How could the guy have just died, as Jack remembered it? And what of Mia's image of Jack hitting the guy's body? Could she really believe he had nothing to do with the man's death?

Mia tossed down her hairbrush and grabbed her jacket from the chair in her room. *Enough. No good is coming from endlessly rewinding the tapes on this stupid disagreement.* She walked into the kitchen and saw he'd poured her a mug of coffee. It sat, the steam wafting off it, on the counter.

"I got an appointment in Lawrenceville," she said to his turned back at the stove.

"What's going on in Lawrenceville?"

"That's where Victoria Baskerville is from."

Jack turned around and made a face. "So you're really going to do this?"

"I told you last night I was taking the case, Jack. Are you going to throw a fit every time I mention it?"

"Nope. Do what you want."

Mia took in a breath and let it out. "You seeing your lawyer today?"

"Mia, I really don't want to discuss it with you."

Okay, now that is downright petulant.

"Fine. See you tonight." Mia turned and snatched her car keys as she headed for the door. A part of her realized that maybe she was behaving a little petulantly herself.

An hour and a car full of Coldplay at top volume later, Mia drove into the modest middle-class subdivision and began looking for the house number that her GPS system assured her was where she wanted to go.

A brief conversation by phone with Peterson had given her the twins' contact information. She'd go by the attorney's office later to pick up her retainer and any other files he thought she should have. The closest thing to Victoria at this point, however, was the twins.

Mia parked on the street in front of an aging split-level with a carport instead of a garage. February was wet and cold in Atlanta and Mia wore a warm rain jacket against the possibility the sky would open up. It definitely looked like it was thinking about it.

The front door opened as she walked up the cracked sidewalk.

"You the detective?"

A teenage girl stood in the doorway. Mia recognized her from the photos in the file—the ones where she was romping in her undies with that sleazeball, Cook. She was blonde, thin, her hair stringy and limp, but clean. As Mia got closer, she saw the girl's face was spotty.

Mia nodded and smiled. "That's me," she said. She reached out her hand as soon as she crossed the threshold. Her people-touching skills were inconclusive at best, but you never knew. The girl pumped Mia's hand in an enthusiastic handshake. Mia felt agitation in her. But that could be because she was about to miss her favorite reality show.

Another girl, nearly identical, showed up behind the first.

"I'm Stacy," she said. "This is Tracy. You the detective?"

"I am," Mia said moving into the house. The air smelled sour and Mia was tempted to breathe through her mouth. But that wasn't what real detectives did. They didn't shy away from gross smells, but noted everything and saw where any of it might fit into the puzzle.

A seriously obese woman materialized from the couch in the living room. At first, Mia thought the whole couch was erupting, until the flowery blouse of the woman separated from the flowered pattern of the sofa. One of the girls ran to help the woman to her feet.

"I'm sorry," the woman said, her voice gasping as if the effort to stand had exhausted her. "I don't know how to pronounce your name. I'm Rhonda Kilpatrick."

"Ms. Kilpatrick," Mia said. "You don't have to get up for me, ma'am."

"Oh, I love your Southern manners, honey," Rhonda wheezed, then collapsed back onto the couch. "Tracy, angel, get that tray of sweet tea in the kitchen."

Tracy bounced off and Mia found an armchair in the living room facing the couch.

"I'm so glad you could meet with me today, Ms. Kilpatrick," Mia said, trying to look around the room without appearing rude. From her notes, she knew Rhonda Kilpatrick was divorced, unemployed and on disability. Obviously the obesity was her disability. If the woman couldn't easily get off the couch, she would likely have trouble doing basic things like commuting and walking up and down stairs.

Tracy brought in a tray of glasses and a pitcher of dark amber tea.

"It's really the girls I was hoping to speak with," Mia said, accepting a sweaty glass of tea from Tracy. "I wanted to know more about Victoria and—"

"Oh, we've known Vickie since we was babies, huh, Stacy?" Tracy said, collapsing on the couch with her tea. "Mama, can we get them cookies out?"

"By all means, Tracy, darlin'," Rhonda said.

Mia was about to say *none for me* when it occurred to her that showing any sign of willpower might be taken as a judgment. She turned to Stacy as Tracy ran from the room again.

"She used to babysit you?"

Stacy nodded her head. "She was more like a big sister," she said, her bottom lip quivering. "I don't like to talk about Vickie because…of what happened."

"Sure. Of course. Can I ask how old you are?" Mia said.

"We're twenty-one," Stacy said. "We look younger."

Mia glanced at Rhonda, but the woman was looking sadly at Stacy.

So Peterson was right. They weren't underage. Just bait.

"You and Vickie were all so close," Mia said, prompting Stacy.

"Oh! Are you talking about Vickie?" Tracy asked as she entered the room with a box of fat-free fudge cookies. "Oh my God, we nearly died, didn't we, Stace? When we found out?"

Stacy reached for a cookie. Rhonda reached for four.

"She would never let anyone hurt us," Stacy said quietly. "She always sent us out of the room before things got…carried away."

"Do you think the guy the cops have…Joshua Cook. Do you think he could have hurt Vickie?" Mia asked.

Tracy shrugged and looked at Stacy, as if waiting for her to answer first.

"He was just a perv," Stacy said. "Giggled a lot. Didn't act like a murderer. But what do I know?"

Mia turned back to Rhonda, who was brushing crumbs off her vast chest.

"So you knew Victoria pretty well, I guess?" Mia asked.

"Oh, my yes," Rhonda said, her cheeks red, her eyes focused on the cookie box on the table. "She sat for my girls since they were infants. Right after the divorce I worked two jobs, you know."

"Wow," Mia said. "That's a lot."

"Well, it's what I had to do to keep the family together."

The twins were now seated next to each other, their hands intertwined. Stacy was staring into space. Tracy was actively listening to Mia and her mother.

"Do you have other children?" Mia asked.

"My older boy, Derek," Rhonda said. "He's at work right now."

"Did Victoria babysit him, too?"

Rhonda and Tracy burst out laughing.

"Oh, my goodness, no," Rhonda said. "My Derek was always a handful and he's not that much younger than Vickie."

"Did they ever…date?"

A look of nausea came over Rhonda's face. "Absolutely not."

That means yes.

"I'd love to talk to Derek, too," Mia said. "Maybe when he gets home from work?"

"I'm afraid that won't be possible. Tracy, put the tea back in the fridge before it drips water all over the coffee table. I'm so sorry Ms…well, I still don't know how to pronounce your name, but we are due at church in an hour and we'll need to get ready."

"Church?" Tracy blurted before Stacy kicked her into silence.

Mia stood. "Would it be okay if I called again?"

"I'd rather you didn't," Rhonda said, brushing lint off her blouse and not looking at Mia. "We've already cooperated with the police and we would just like to put this whole unfortunate situation behind us. Thank you for respecting our privacy."

"Of course." Mia smiled at the twins but only Tracy returned her smile. She went to the door and was about to thank them again for seeing her when she spotted a young man on the street walking around her car.

Could this be Derek?

She hurried down the sidewalk toward him. She noticed he was dressed in a dirty T-shirt and ripped jeans. So clearly his job wasn't bagging at the local Kroger.

"This your car?" he asked as she approached. He was blond like his sisters and mother, but scrawny and ill-looking. She could see his bad teeth from twenty feet away. Meth teeth. In his hand, he carried a short metal pipe.

"I was just visiting your sisters and mother," Mia said breathlessly. The man reeked of menace.

"Derek!" Stacy called from the porch. "Mama said you to come in right this minute!"

"That pervert's lawyer done sent you, didn't he?" Derek said, addressing her car more than Mia.

She worried the whole drive over that the family might not want to talk with her when they found out her purpose—to find proof of the prime suspect's innocence in killing their beloved Vickie. It hadn't occurred to her they might want to bash her head in with a metal pipe.

"I am just leaving," Mia said. But she didn't move. Derek stood between her and the car.

"And you ain't never coming back, right?" Derek said, turning on her.

Mia took an involuntary step backward just as he swung the pipe full force into the windshield of her car. She stumbled and fell on the sidewalk, the sound of the pipe falling to the cement and the twins' screams behind her, ringing in her ears.

*****

Jack kept one eye on the kitchen timer. The pear chutney would be just as good cold as warm but the pork chops wouldn't. He probably should have held off putting them in the hot skillet until after calling his attorney.

Something about maybe going to jail that screws with your timing.

"Okay, Jack, there's a civil suit now," Paul Murray said.

Jack sat heavily on the stool at the kitchen counter, his phone in his hand. Mia wasn't home yet. His shoulders slumped.

"Yeah, well. One thing at a time," he said glancing at the oven clock. The pork chops were spitting and hissing in the pan. "When's the preliminary hearing?"

"Next week. Tuesday."

Jack let out a long sigh.

"I wish you'd let me cut a deal, Jack. This could get messy. It doesn't have to go down like this."

"And I wish you'd just do your job."

"Keeping you out of prison is my job."

"No deals. I didn't murder the son of a bitch."

"Yeah, okay, Jack. Let me get back to you."

Jack hung up and went to the stove in time to turn the chops. He stared at them sizzling in the pan, trying to enjoy the moment he always got when he was cooking—the flow that helped him transcend mortal concerns and pains.

Not today.

He removed the chops to a dish and slid it into the warm oven, then scraped the chutney into the still-hot pan.

Can this really be happening? The thought of doing jail time—let alone *prison* time—was literally something that wouldn't compute in his brain. And for what? For attempting to restrain someone from cutting Mia's throat? Isn't that all he did?

Jack looked up from the pan and tried to remember for the thousandth time what had happened that night. He remembered the riotous, overwhelming fear when he saw Mia in that bastard's hands, the knife glinting in the harsh security light overhead—the knife that pressed into her beautiful throat. Yes, he remembered the fury that coursed through him. It took everything he had not to lunge at the man right then, which almost certainly would have ended with Mia dead.

Instead, he focused on the guy's eyes to get that telltale moment that would alert Jack to what the guy was about to do. It was usually no more than a blink or a shift in gaze, but if you were looking for it, it was unmistakable. And when he saw it, when he saw the guy momentarily distracted by something out of the corner of his eye, Jack moved. Two steps and he had the knife hand solidly in his own. Then a twist to the wrist, and he'd forced him to drop the knife.

What then? The knife was on the ground. And the sound of it hitting the ground was also the sound of the self-defense plea falling off the table with a resounding thud.

Jack remembered pushing Mia away so he could deal with the guy without her between them.

Wasn't he still furious? Did he even really remember what happened next? Isn't it true that all he remembered was the frenzy that seemed to swallow up his whole world? Had he wanted to hit the guy? Pummel him senseless?

Beat the life out of him?

Jack turned off the skillet, no longer hungry. Mia said she saw Jack whaling away on the guy's lifeless form. The partial frame the security cameras caught hinted at a similar telling of events.

Is that what happened? It was certainly what Jack had *wanted* to happen. The guy was definitely dead. Can you *will* someone dead?

He went to the fridge and pulled out a cold beer. Mia only liked domestics, and Jack had been unsuccessful so far in getting her to try any imported ales. He cracked open the beer and went to the living room. Usually Daisy was right at his feet when Jack cooked, hoping for a dropped tidbit. Tonight she lay curled up on the couch like she could sense his mood.

"Did I kill him?" Jack asked out loud. The dog cocked her head at the sound of his voice. He took a long pull on his beer. "I wanted to," he whispered.

He glanced at his hands, one holding the bottle, and felt a sickening feeling begin to radiate through his chest. Tonight, all he could remember with any certainty was his anger—the uncontrolled, holy fury of his anger.

In the end, maybe that's all there was. *That and a dead guy who'd threatened to hurt the one person I love most in the world.*

*****

Tad had left his lunch behind on the counter again. Mindy looked at it from where she sat at the kitchen table. This wasn't the first time he'd forgotten it. Was it intentional? Was he really so clueless he couldn't remember the lunch she'd packed for him?

Mindy fought the urge to grab the paper bag and shred it over her husband's bed pillow.

Think he'd remember to bring it next time if he had to sleep in tuna salad and wilted lettuce leaves tonight?

She forced herself not to look at the lunch bag. But when she looked away from it, she came back to the issue at hand. Specifically, a notecard with matching envelope that came in the mail that morning. The card itself was embossed with a large loopy letter K. In contrast, the handwriting on the card was spare and minimalistic, as if trying to make up for the ornate watermark.

"*Dear Mindy, Thank you so much for calling the other day. I hope we find an opportunity soon to get together. I'm looking forward to getting to know you, and your mother, too. Meanwhile, know that you're in my thoughts. Best wishes and love, Jess Kazmaroff.*"

Mindy took the notecard and propped it against the saltshaker on the kitchen table as she opened up her laptop. In the hour since the mail had come, she had to admit she'd gone from feeling extremely upset—*is the woman mocking me?*—to feeling as if she'd been unknowingly waiting for this opportunity all along. She opened her browser and cracked her knuckles. Tad made fun of her when she sat down to a computer, as well he might. The man was a total ignoramus when it came to technology. He never updated his smartphone software unless she nagged him to, and half the time complained that he then had to relearn how to use it.

When Mindy opened her laptop she felt what she imagined master chess players or progeny pianists felt when they sat down to play. It was that moment when a feeling of peace and fulfillment, combined with a sense of order and rightness, settled on her like gently falling confetti.

It was hard not to know exactly when her life had changed. The first time she knew she had a gift for computers was right about the time she started doing poorly in school. It was also hard not to remember the look of horror and disappointment from her father during that time—a time of discovery and enlightenment for her that collided painfully with the first steps of estrangement from him.

I wonder if it's always like that? When you find the thing that makes you come alive, does it kill all those other things in your life you thought you needed?

What followed her revelations in middle school and high school was a series of problems—and two arrests—that for Mindy were as impossible to avoid as breathing. But still her father couldn't see that. Didn't he think she'd stop if she could? Didn't he know how she wanted to please him? Why couldn't he understand?

Hacking was the only thing that made sense to her.

Her phone vibrated and she glanced at it. A picture of her husband materialized on the screen and she smiled fondly at it…and pressed *Decline*.

Not now, my love. I have work to do.

She picked up the phone and snapped a picture of Jess's notecard—Jess's very thoughtful, very timely notecard—and smiled.

6

Mia handed her car keys to the body shop manager and picked up the keys to her rental car. It was going to be interesting explaining a broken windshield to Jack. He was clearly in no mood these days to think it wasn't completely her fault.

What the hell was the deal with Derek? Was he just a psycho? Should she try to question him?

She drove to Midtown, checking her phone to see if Jack had called—he hadn't—and found the law offices of Bentley & Jamison. It was located in the Midtown Business District, a block away from the Woodruff Arts Center, a landmark building most people thought defined the Atlanta skyline.

Mia just thought it was going to be a major pain in the ass to find a parking spot.

When she finally did—on the ninth floor of the parking garage in the same building—she tucked the parking ticket into her bag, praying they validated, and found her way to the lobby of the famous building. She reached the lobby and spotted George Peterson standing by the security desk waiting for her.

"I hope I'm not late," she said. She knew she was at least thirty minutes late.

"Not at all," Peterson said, smiling at her and reaching out to shake hands. "Let's sit over here, shall we?" To the right of the elevators, he indicated a closed door Mia hadn't noticed. Inside there was a couch, cocktail table and conference table. Mia went to the sofa and sank into the thick cushions.

"Thank you for taking the case," Peterson said, handing Mia a long white envelope. "Your retainer."

Mia tucked the envelope away without opening it. "Thank you."

"I have a few more files for you and a visitation set up with our client in about five minutes."

Mia frowned. "Cook is coming here? He's out?"

"No, it's a web-based video visitation system." Peterson opened up the laptop on the coffee table and typed in his password. "I think it will suffice for you getting a read on him. Frankly," he looked at her and shrugged, "I'm not sure meeting him in any form will benefit you, but then, you've already agreed to take the case, haven't you?"

Not for your client's sake, I haven't.

"That's right," Mia said.

"Can I ask what made you change your mind?"

"Mostly the money."

Peterson narrowed his eyes, as if trying to determine if she were joking. Finally, he said, "I heard about your partner. His arrest."

"Do you know his lawyer?"

Peterson nodded. "Paul Murray. He's good. He'll give him good advice. Whether your partner's smart enough to take it, of course, is another matter."

"Can I ask you what evidence they have against Cook?"

"I have all that for you," Peterson said as he handed her a stack of file folders. "Plus a list of the men Ms. Baskerville contacted but whom were not considered suspects."

He handed her a sheaf of pages stapled together. "Ms. Baskerville's diary. Nothing obviously incriminating to anyone. Mostly just her thoughts about life."

Mia took the folders and the notebook and slid them into her shoulder bag.

"As for the evidence, Cook admitted he was at the scene of the crime."

"He did?"

"Yes. The treads of his sneakers were coated in the victim's blood. He arrived several hours after she was attacked. He went there hoping to convince her to give him the pictures. You'll see in his statement that he found the victim's door wide open."

"Pretty damning."

"You'll also see in the files a statement from our medical expert confirming the wounds were delivered by a left-handed person."

"Is Cook?"

"He's right-handed."

"That wasn't enough to make the cops fall out of love with him as a suspect?"

"They felt, compared with everything else, it was a minor detail that could be explained away."

"Meaning it's your job to make it look like a very big detail to the jury," Mia said.

"Let's hope it doesn't get that far. Oh. He's logging on now." Peterson turned back to the laptop.

Mia leaned forward to stare at the screen, which suddenly filled with the seated form of a man wearing an orange jumpsuit. Late thirties, pale ginger hair and facial stubble, and watery blue eyes. He looked into the camera with an arrogance that belied where he was broadcasting from.

"Hello, Josh," Peterson said to the screen. "I'd like you to meet Mia Kazmaroff, from the detective firm of Burton & Kazmaroff. She's agreed to help us." He turned to Mia. "You can ask him anything you like. Isn't that right, Josh?"

"As long as I can ask her a few things about what she's wearing under that dumpy T-shirt," Cook said.

"I thought you only liked kids," Mia said.

"You can't say things like that," Peterson hissed. "This is taped."

"Yeah, great, Peterson," Cook said. "Did you hire this bitch from the prosecution side?"

"I've seen enough," Mia said, gathering up the file folder Peterson had set on the couch between them.

"Are...are you sure?" Peterson said.

"Yes. I'll read the files and call you if I have any questions."

"Would you like to meet me in person, sweetheart? Because that can be arranged."

"I'll be in touch," Mia said, standing and hurrying toward the door. Peterson stood but didn't follow her. When she closed the door behind her, before bolting for the elevators and the parking garage, she hesitated, then turned back to the closed door. No sound was audible from the other side. She touched the doorknob and felt... nothing.

Either the lawyer was a cyborg or he really had no strong feelings about the case one way or the other.

Somehow, that made Mia feel worse.

*****

An hour later, Mia was still in Midtown. Hoping to avoid the crush of traffic hemorrhaging out of downtown to the suburban hinterlands, she texted Jack that she would be a no-show for dinner. She grabbed a fast-food burger and found a park bench in Centennial Park. If it had been a touch chillier—or wetter—she would've fought the surly knot of homeless for a spot in the Fulton County library off Margaret Mitchell Square, but as it was the weather was still passable.

She spread out the file folder Peterson had given her and ate her dinner while skimming his interviews and notes. When she saw the page on Nathan Turner, the CEO of *Atlanta Loves*, the online dating service that Victoria used, she punched in the private number listed and was surprised when he picked up.

"I'm a detective hired by the firm defending Joshua Cook," she said, brushing hamburger bun crumbs from her jeans. "I'm downtown at the moment. Would you happen to have a moment to meet with me? I promise to be quick."

He hesitated. "May I ask your name?"

"Mia Kazmaroff, of Burton & Kazmaroff Detective Agency."

"Do you know where I am located?"

"I do."

"Thirty minutes?"

"That's great. Thank you."

The picture of Turner in the file revealed a handsome man in his mid forties. He was smiling into the camera and Mia wondered if this was his online dating profile picture. She couldn't find any personal information on him to show whether he was married, straight or gay.

She shivered at the memory of her meeting with Joshua Cook. It wasn't that he was more repugnant than she expected. He was right on the money in that regard. It was his surpassing arrogance at the whole situation.

Child molesters weren't treated well in prison if the stories could be believed. Either he was the coolest individual ever created, or he had special reason to believe he would not be going down for Victoria's murder.

Mia wadded up her trash and headed for the nearest receptacle. It made more sense to walk the five blocks down Peachtree Street to the offices of *Atlanta Loves* than maneuver her rental car through downtown traffic. It took her ten minutes but she was comfortably warm by the time she punched the elevator button in Nathan Turner's office building in Colony Square.

A beautiful redhead sat at the receptionist's desk off the elevator. Mia was surprised support staff would be working this late.

"I'm here to see Nathan Turner," Mia said, suddenly feeling frumpy and disheveled next to the immaculately dressed young woman.

The receptionist spoke into her headset and then turned to Mia. "He said he'll meet you halfway." She nodded toward the hallway and Mia thanked her.

He did a little better than halfway. Before Mia even opened the door to the hall, he was standing there, his hand out to shake hers, a strained smile on his face.

"Ms. Kazmaroff, welcome," he said, shaking her hand.

"Mr. Turner. Thank you for seeing me so last minute."

Nathan Turner was very tall and very blond, with a thick mustache giving him a striking appearance that was hard to ignore. She imagined that was the point.

"Not at all," he said. "Let's meet in here." He indicated a room ahead of them. Inside, Mia was impressed with the number of video screens on the wall and on nearly every flat surface in the room.

"I was happy to help the police in this terrible business," Turner said, holding a chair out for Mia to sit at the conference table. "So I don't know what more I can answer."

"Well, my questions might be a little different from theirs," Mia said, shrugging out of her coat, "since they want to prove my client's client killed Ms. Baskerville, and my job is to show he didn't."

"I see. Of course. Ask away."

Mia glanced around the room. Several of the wall-mounted screens played video clips of what looked like happy couples on their wedding days, presumably the result of successful matching by *Atlanta Loves*.

"Can you tell me how the police knew of Mr. Cook's existence?"

"I'm not a physician or a priest, Ms. Kazmaroff. I have no special protection. The police requested that information from me and since I wanted to help, I gave it."

"Without a warrant?"

"That's right."

"What, exactly, did you give them?"

Turner sighed and ran a hand over his face, as if the answer to that was too monumental to tackle. "I gave them the names of those members with whom Ms. Baskerville had Stage Three contact."

"Stage Three contact?"

"That means beyond the initial contact. A good number of our male members felt they were a strong match for Ms. Baskerville. She was beautiful and her profile indicated she was open to more...adventurous sorts of romantic liaisons."

"So let me understand how this works. A woman puts her profile up on your site and waits until a guy sees it and indicates he's interested?"

"That's right."

"She can't just pluck his profile out of the slush pile and contact him?"

"No, she has to be selected first."

"Pretty sexist."

"Our women clients like it that way. Makes them feel more feminine. More Southern."

"If you say so. Then once she gets notified that some guy is interested in her profile, she's at Stage One?"

"Correct. Stage Two would be an exchange of some kind between them as they get to know each other in order to decide if they want to take it farther."

"And the cops were only interested in those men who made it to Stage Three?"

"Yes. Only those men who received a message from Ms. Baskerville, recorded in our system, releasing her phone number or personal email."

"With the intention of arranging a meeting."

"Presumably. After that, it's out of my hands."

"How many Stage Threes did you have for her?"

"About two hundred."

Mia whistled. "And they found Cook out of that haystack? Good job, Atlanta PD."

"Good job assuming they got the right man," Turner said.

"Which brings us to now. You don't know *how* they winnowed the number down from two hundred to Joshua Cook?" *Aside from the fact that he was walking around in her blood the day she was murdered.*

"I understand they were able to do it through a number of phone interviews. Not all of the men ended up meeting with her so, of course, the police ruled them out until they had just those who agreed to her invitation to meet her two little friends."

"The underage girls."

"I had no idea she was doing anything like that."

"What about the Stage Ones and Twos? Do you have a list of that group in your database?"

Turner frowned. "Of course. But it must be over a thousand men. Maybe more."

"I'll need a copy of their names and contact information."

"Really? Is that legal?"

"Absolutely," Mia said, not at all sure if it was legal or not. "This case is officially *closed*, Mr. Turner. The cops have their man."

"I see." Turner tapped his pen—an expensive fountain pen from the looks of it—against the conference room table.

"So, all total, you have a thousand men who contacted her. And you're sure there's no way of going on to Stage Two without you knowing?

"That is correct."

"Do you have copies of their communication with Ms. Baskerville?"

"Of course."

"And the cops never asked you for it?"

"They probably didn't think it was worth following up on."

"Well, that's what I'm counting on anyway."

"I'm impressed, Ms. Kazmaroff. You must believe strongly in your client's innocence to wade though the transcripts of one thousand men."

"Mr. Cook isn't my client," Mia said stiffly. "Can I ask you, merely for my own information, what you told the police when they asked for your whereabouts the night Ms. Baskerville was killed?"

"You may," he said. "But you might not like the answer."

"They never asked you."

He shrugged. "The police are extremely busy, Ms. Kazmaroff. You can't blame them for failing to ask for alibis from non-suspects. That would be a monumental waste of time, don't you think?"

Something about the way Turner delivered that line made Mia shiver—even in the warm, climate-controlled office building.

*****

Jack stood in the living room of the Atlantic Station condo and stared out the picture window at Atlanta's skyline. The phone had rung a few times but he'd let it go to voice mail. The file his lawyer sent over sat open on the dining room table.

Jim Martin, age forty-two. The photograph in the file was an employee photo taken the day Martin joined the fire extinguisher company. He was smiling in it. Smiling like he expected good things to come from his new employment. Smiling like he thought it was the beginning of a better life.

The picture was taken less than six months ago.

Jack had killed people before—in the military, and in the line of duty during fourteen years as a police officer. His stomach lurched painfully. He'd never killed anyone with his bare hands. And never in the grip of uncontrollable anger.

Is that what happened? Did my actions bring about Martin's death?

Would the guy still be alive if he hadn't bumped into Jack that night? Jack ran both hands across his face and felt the horror of the words seep into his shoulders, his neck, and creep up into his brain.

Is this what love does to you? Makes you crazy? Makes you willing to commit murder? Or is this only how love affects me?

He heard Mia's key in the door and forced himself to move away from the window to greet her. It wasn't her fault she saw him for exactly who he was.

"Hey," she said as she dropped her car keys on the table at the door. "Did you get my texts?"

"Yeah, I didn't cook tonight." That was partially true. The cooked pork chops were wrapped, in the refrigerator.

"Oh, good. You didn't answer so I didn't know."

"I've had a few things on my mind, Mia."

"I know." She began peeling off her coat. "Any news?"

"Preliminary hearing is Tuesday."

"Why so soon? Don't you get to push it back?"

"I don't see any point. The guy's family is mounting a civil suit against me."

"Shit." Mia walked to the dining room table and picked up the folder with Martin's picture. Jack took the file from her.

"If you're hungry, I can make you a sandwich."

"Jack, stop it. I don't want a sandwich. I want us to talk."

"About your day? Sure. I'm all ears. Have a nice visit with the child molester?"

Her mouth dropped open and he hated the look on her face. He turned away.

"What is your problem?" she said.

"My problem, Mia, is that I'm likely going to prison in a few months for killing a guy whose only crime was making a poor decision at work."

"Is that what they call holding a knife to my throat?"

"I'm charged with using undue force," he said, feeling his voice heat up. "And you, yourself, confirm that."

"Do you really want me to lie to you, Jack? Is that what this relationship needs to survive? Me telling you what you need to hear?"

"No, you're right. I'd much rather have a relationship with someone who thinks I killed a guy with my bare hands."

"I don't know what to tell you, Jack. This relationship wouldn't be worth having if I felt I had to lie to you."

Tears clung to her lashes and her lips trembled as she spoke and somehow, perversely, it made him feel better. He was inches from drawing her into his arms and erasing her pain, her shock and her hurt when, irrationally, he found himself striding to the door and snatching his car keys.

Truth was, he couldn't bear to look at her complete disappointment in him another moment.

7

Mia rolled over and squinted at the digital clock on her bedside stand. She didn't need to peek in Jack's bedroom to know he hadn't come home last night. There was an undisturbed quiet about the place that told her that without looking.

She'd cried after he left and then counted the minutes, hoping he would come back and they would finally break through to each other. But the minutes turned into hours, the cable shows became infomercials and she eventually dragged herself to bed.

It's just a fight. People have them all the time. He's under a lot of stress. He's just lashing out.

She showered and dressed, made herself a single cup of coffee and opened up her laptop. No emails needing immediate action. A few new photos on Facebook uploaded the night before by Jess: one of Mia and Ned clowning in the dressing room of the wedding boutique; one of Maxwell, asleep in a lounge chair at Jess's, his reading glasses on his nose, a book collapsed across his chest.

Her phone chimed to announce the receipt of a text message. Glancing at the screen, she saw that her car was ready at the body shop.

I wonder if Jack even noticed it was missing from the parking lot? She tried to focus on her work and logged onto *Atlanta Loves* using the account she'd opened for herself. Without sending out any probes, she created a profile and quickly ran through the protocol for how the site worked. Then she set up the sheets of men's names Nathan Turner had given her and typed the first one in the search box. It brought up the guy's profile.

Dennis Kraus, age thirty, teaches at Georgia State University. The picture showed a man in his late twenties. Mia flipped through the transcripts that showed his conversation with Victoria—brief and to the point.

Victoria: <Thanks for the interest.>

Kraus: <Sure. I liked your picture. Very cute.>

That was it. For some reason, there was no more contact between them. Mia sighed and hefted the sheaf of names in her hand. It was going to take a very long time to check out all the dead ends. Welcome to the exciting world of detective work. She got up to get a Coke out of the fridge and, on impulse, picked up her phone and called Ned.

He answered on the third ring.

"Hey," Mia said. "Got a minute?"

"Uh, sure."

"I just need to bounce an idea or two off you. I'd do it with my mom but she's squeamish about me hanging out with murderers and pedophiles."

"Imagine that."

"Okay. First, I've got a total sleezoid who had opportunity *and* motive—"

"Is he the guy in custody?" Ned asked.

"Yes. And he's the poster child for this murder. Fits it perfectly, but here's where it gets weird. There are a few other people who might fit it nearly as perfectly."

"Ooh, profiling. I've heard the police do that."

"Well, anyway," Mia continued, "I went to meet the twins who were in on the scam with Victoria and they don't look like they had enough brain cells between them to have killed her, plus my gut tells me they loved her and didn't do it."

"I'll remind you that your gut doesn't hold up in court."

"But their brother, Derek, is a psychopath and I can think of all kinds of reasons why *he* might have wanted to hurt Victoria. First, he's violent, and there's a rumor that he and Victoria were an item."

"Plus she was pimping out his sisters, which might also have been a problem for him."

"Exactly," Mia said. "I don't know how I'm going to get his alibi, but from the files I got from my client—Cook's lawyer—the cops didn't even interview him."

"Slack."

"Then there's the head of the online dating service, a real iceman called Nathan Turner."

"I know him," Ned said.

"Okay, what?"

"I know him. He's very big in the gay community. Kind of a dick but kind of cool, too, and a philanthropist."

"That is so strange, Ned. Really?"

"You didn't pick up on that?"

"Him being gay? No. Him having a secret? Big time."

"What's his motive?"

"I don't know, do I? Maybe it's attached to whatever his secret is," she said.

"Did you touch him?"

"I couldn't find a natural way to do it."

"I'm proud of you, Mia. Shows real self-restraint."

"I've also got the files on a guy who was on the cops' runner-up list. I'm going to meet him this morning."

"He look good for it?"

"Hard to tell," she said. "He got scammed by her."

"That's motive."

"Where are you?" Mia asked. "Are the maids there? I hear clanging in the background. And cursing."

"Yes, the maids are here as a matter of fact. Gee, you must be a detective. Are we finished?"

"I guess so. Jack stormed out last night after a big fight and didn't come home."

"Really."

"It was a *very* big fight, Ned. Things got said. One thing led to another."

"They always do. I'm sure he's just licking his wounds somewhere. You guys'll sort it out. Listen, Mia, I gotta go. You going to be okay?"

"Yeah, sure. Thanks, Ned. Oh, by the way, please tell Jack he better come home soon if he doesn't want me to use all his fancy cheeses to make grilled sandwiches with. I know he hates that."

"Bye, Mia."

"Bye."

*****

"What'd she say?" Jack asked as Ned hung up the phone.

"I hate doing this shit. Can't you two just talk it out?"

"And say what? *Don't see what you think you saw?* There's nothing to say. Besides, it's not the end of the world."

"Well it kinda is if you go to prison, Jack."

Jack handed Ned a steaming mug of coffee and sat down on the sofa in Ned's comfortable Morningside cottage. It hadn't occurred to him when he made his dramatic exit from Mia's last night that he really had no place to go. He'd known Ned—really Mia's friend—all of six months. It *did* occur to him that the first smile he'd had in forty-eight hours was from the look on Ned's face when he opened his door last night and found Jack standing on his doorstep.

"Can I run something by you?" Jack asked.

"That seems to be my function this morning," Ned said, going to the kitchen to add more cream to his coffee. "I assume I am in the role of Priest Confidant? Listen but keep my mouth shut?"

"I just need to walk through it one time in the light of day, without Mia over my shoulder, or my lawyer trying to twist the facts into something that will work in my favor."

"I'm happy to help, Jack. Seriously." Ned joined him on the couch. "And I promise not to tell Mia."

"Thank you." Jack focused his mind. He'd slept little last night.

"I remember being absolutely poleaxed to see Mia on the other side of the fence. Like it was a bad LSD trip."

"You've done acid?"

"No, Ned. I'm just telling you how unbelievable it was to me to see her there. She was supposed to be coming back from the Jiffy Mart. For a few seconds, I just didn't comprehend what I was seeing."

"Understandable."

"When I realized it really was her, I climbed the fence and made it to the other side in time to see the guy with his hands on Mia ..."

Jack stopped, as if seeing the image in his head. He exhaled harshly and shook his head to compose himself. "I don't even remember what he said. I saw the knife and I saw Mia's eyes. So big and afraid." He swallowed.

"That must have been terrible," Ned said quietly.

"Yeah. It was. I wanted to rush him but I waited until he looked away for a second and then I wrenched the knife from him."

Jack didn't speak for a moment. He was remembering the pure relief of knowing the knife was no longer at her throat. That she was safe. The adrenaline that had been surging through him seemed to have ebbed.

"I pushed her away and he slugged me. I was happy to let him go and have the cops pick him up later. Really." He glanced at Ned to see his reaction but Ned just nodded for him to continue.

"But he had no intention of running. He pulled back his fist to hit me again and I blocked it with my forearm. I punched him. Maybe twice. I can't remember. He looked down where the knife was and I tackled him to the ground."

"That must have been when the surveillance cameras lost you."

"I guess. But when I had him on the ground, he went limp. I thought he might be faking it."

"You think he died then?"

"Or was in the process. I remember slapping him but he was unresponsive so I started doing chest compressions. I was angry and maybe I did them harder than necessary. The ME says I ruptured his spleen."

"Yeah, but if he was already dying *before* you gave him CPR then the spleen thing wasn't what killed him."

"How the hell do I prove that? And as long as it's my word against forensics, I'm dead."

"You need to tell Mia this."

"I *told* her, Ned. I know she's trying to believe in me but what guy just stops breathing for no reason?"

"Jack. The prosecution sees *you* as the reason he stopped breathing because they don't have another possibility. It's your job—or your attorney's—to give them another one."

"What the hell could that be? I was there, and even *I* have trouble believing I didn't kill him. And Mia definitely does."

"Mia saw you hit him. She was already freaked out so when the guy ended up dead, she put two and two together and got ninety-four."

"If I'd just taken the guy's knife and told him to beat it—"

"You said yourself he wasn't interested in running. He *wanted* a confrontation."

"All I know is I mishandled the situation. And now he's dead."

"You know anything about him?"

Jack shook his head. "Just somebody trying to get a little more out of a shitty life. Plus, however desperate or stupid he was to steal from his employer—"

"And hold a woman at knifepoint, don't forget."

"Yeah, that too. But in spite of all that, he obviously has family who cares. They're bringing a civil suit against me."

"Maybe they're just trying to get money out of the city?"

"I don't work for the city any more. And if they're trying to get money out of *me*, they're in for a rude surprise."

"Your lawyer know everything you told me today?"

"Of course."

"And he doesn't think you stand a good chance at an acquittal?"

"He thinks we should ask for a deal."

"Will that include prison time?"

"Oh, yeah."

*****

Mia parked two blocks over from Colony Square in Midtown. It was lunch hour in the heart of Atlanta's ad agency enclave. The sidewalks were crowded with streams of office workers coming and going from the area eateries. She glanced at the small photograph she had of Barry Cargill, agency account executive from Mod2, a creative boutique specializing in medical animation and health services advertising.

From the photo, he looked sincere and friendly—exactly the look you'd want to project if your job was to woo clients for your agency. Hair a little wispy on top but a pleasant, relaxed face.

He was also prime suspect number two behind Cook for Victoria Baskerville's murder. If the cops hadn't had bloody sneaker treads with Cook's name on them, Mr. Cargill would be sitting in a maximum-security holding pen right now instead of choosing his next sushi lunch venue.

Mia walked south from 10th Street toward what was generally considered the advertising crowd's most popular lunchtime destination, Hobson's Tavern, just west of Peachtree Street. Her preference was to catch Cargill away from the office and she'd allotted two days of staking out Hobson's to achieve that. But her fallback was a frontal attack on the agency itself in the guise of a durable medical equipment rep. She knew Cargill was in town—she'd called earlier to confirm that. If she didn't catch him today or tomorrow, she'd have to do it the hard way and get an appointment.

As she walked, she tried to let the cooler air—even the dampness, which frizzed her hair—energize her. She knew Jack was at Ned's. She hadn't really been sure about that until Ned answered. But something about his hesitancy and then too-prompt replies broadcast the fact that he was keeping a secret—a six-foot four, one hundred and eighty pound secret.

That was good. Ned would help calm Jack down, maybe even talk some sense into him. Her phone vibrated and she pulled it out of her jacket pocket, surprised to see it was a text from Jack.

<I'm sorry for acting like a dick. Forgive me?>

A flood of relief cascaded through her and she stopped on the sidewalk to type in her answer. <Of course. You okay?>

<Better.>

<See u tonight?>

<Got a gig until late.>

<I'll wait up.>

<Good.>

Mia tucked her phone away and grinned. *How the world can change from one moment to the next when you're in love.*

She saw a group of people standing in line to get into Hobson's Tavern and scanned the crowd for Cargill. Beginning to doubt the plausibility of her ambush plan, Mia pushed into the throng at the door and found herself in front of a harried woman wearing a low-cut silk blouse and armed with a clipboard.

"Name?" she said.

"I think my party's already inside," Mia said.

The woman stepped aside for Mia to pass. Once inside the dining room, Mia was certain her plan was flawed. The long mahogany bar that spanned the length of the room was crowded with men in suits—and a few women—perched uncomfortably on barstools. The noise level was deafening. Mia felt her fingertips humming even though she wasn't touching anything. *Nothing like an overstimulated environment to totally swamp a hypersensitive condition.*

Besides, advertising people? Probably half the people in here have cut somebody's throat. Well, figuratively anyway.

She pushed her way farther into the dining room, slowly skirting each table and glancing at the faces. It was with relief and not a little urgency that she exited the restaurant five minutes later. It had started to rain but being outside was still more comfortable than the stifling and noisy interior of the popular bistro.

Screw it. She'd grab a burrito on the way home and make an appointment to see Cargill in his office later in the week. As soon as she resolved her next course of action, Mia saw him. He was at the end of the line of people waiting to get in, talking with two other men in suits. He looked only vaguely like the man in the photograph she carried.

Seriously bloated—or downright fat—his hair having given up the pretense, and his eyes were mean and piggy, darting back and forth as he spoke.

She half expected to see a little toad tongue flicker out as he spoke.

Beats wasting three hours pretending to be a durable medical equipment rep, she reminded herself as she walked up to him.

"Barry Cargill?" she said.

All three men turned to her.

"I'm Barry Cargill," he said, blatantly raking her from top to toe with an appraising eye.

Really, dude? What if I were a prospective client?

She stuck out her hand. "My name is Mia Kazmaroff. May I have a word?"

He did not shake her hand. And the two men with him quietly drifted ahead in line.

"What about?"

"I bet you know," Mia said cheerfully. "I have a photograph of you taken with some friends of mine I'd like to ask you about."

Cargill's face went slack and he took several steps out of line, prompting Mia to follow him. He looked over his shoulder at his companions but kept walking.

"Mr. Cargill?" Mia walked behind him until he stopped in front of a park bench. The rain was only a mist now and he sat down heavily.

"The cops said they wouldn't make those photographs public. I got a family, you know."

"I'm not with the police."

"Shit! The media?" His face fell into the meaty palms of his hands and Mia nearly felt sorry for him.

"No, not them either." She sat down next to him. He lifted his head to scrutinize her.

"Well, who the fuck are you?"

"Just someone with a few questions. Talk to me and I'll leave you alone."

"What do you want to know?"

Mia dug out a notepad and a pen and handed it to him. "For starters, how well did you know Victoria?"

He held the notepad. "We had one date."

"Where you met the twins."

His lips flattened and his face reddened. "Yes, where I met the fucking twins."

"You must have been pretty upset when she tried to blackmail you."

"Look, whoever you are, I already talked to the cops and they know I was with my wife and her family when the bitch was murdered. I got five people who can testify."

"So your wife knows?"

"She does and she's divorcing me. Anything else?"

"If you would be so kind as to jot down the password for your profile at *Atlanta Loves*."

"I closed that account."

"Well, then it shouldn't be a problem giving me the password."

Mia waited while he stared at her. Finally, he scribbled down a word on the notepad and shoved it back at her.

"Are we done?" He stood without waiting for an answer and strode back in the direction of the offices of Mod2.

Must have lost his appetite.

Mia glanced at the password scrawled on the pad. *Honeys.* A thrill of triumph pierced her. But it wasn't the password that made her feel like she'd done good work today.

It was the fact that Cargill had written it with his left hand.

*****

Jack's car wasn't in the parking lot but she hadn't expected it to be. It was after six. He was probably full swing into the first course of prepping whatever culinary feast he was creating tonight.

Mia rolled her head to ease the tension in her neck. She pulled a beer out of the fridge and settled down on the couch with Daisy and the case file folder, her phone and a notepad. As far as she was concerned, Cook and Cargill were neck and neck for most likely suspect for the murder. Cook had motive plus he was there, tromping around the crime scene, but Cargill had motive *and* he was left-handed, unlike Cook. Obviously, the cops went with the forensic evidence as the easier case to prove.

She jotted down the names—*Cook, Cargill, Derek, Turner*—and stared at them. Derek had a different kind of motive but he had one nonetheless. And Mia didn't know where he was that night. Turner, on the other hand, wasn't an obvious suspect but Mia had picked up on a strong vein of guilt in his manner. She scolded herself for not being more aggressive in touching him. They didn't even shake hands and she could certainly have pushed that.

A text from Jack chimed on her phone.

<Left you a mac and cheese.>

She typed a response. *<You know me so well.>*

<BTW. Love you.>

Mia caught her breath and typed him back.*<Love you 2>*

Feeling her world click back into place, Mia hopped up to find the dish he'd left for her in the refrigerator. She heated it the oven and then fed Daisy. This was her opportunity to show Jack they were a unit and that she believed in him. Jack would open up to her about his case if she stopped reminding him that the emperor was buck naked.

She brought her hot mac and cheese to the couch and settled down with her notes again. Peterson had given her a complete copy of Victoria's diary. Mia was only a few weeks into the entries and felt guilty every time she picked it up for invading the dead woman's privacy. But if Mia knew anything, she knew the only way she was going to get traction on this case was by going down the roads the cops couldn't be bothered to.

Maxwell's words continued to come back to her: not enough resources, time or money to check everything out.

That's where Mia came in. She turned to a recent entry in the diary.

Tuesday, November 15. Why does every holiday remind me of D? You'd think I'd eventually get over that, move on. After everything that's happened.

Mia picked up a highlighter and circled the letter D. Could she be referring to Derek?

Alice called me again today. Wish someone would put her on a leash. She says D wants to know why I don't write him. Is she serious? Ten years ago she would've hunted me down with a blowtorch if I'd sent him so much as a postcard. Am I ever going to be done with those people? I try to imagine what J would say if he knew.

Daisy barked and Mia jumped.

"Way to scare the crap out of me," she said to the dog.

So now who the hell was J? She wrote down the initial on her list of suspects. Maybe something in the files would match up with it. And who's Alice? And what is she afraid of J knowing? Something about "those people."

Mia glanced at the clock. A little after ten. Jack wouldn't be home for another four hours. She closed the file folder and picked up the remote control. She'd gotten in the habit of watching the ten o'clock news most nights. There were a few bites left of her dinner that she let Daisy deal with. As she was cranking up the volume on the TV, a loud thump resounded at her front door. Nearly choking when she heard the noise, Daisy let out a strangled bark and flung herself off the couch.

Mia got up cautiously and followed the dog, who was now barking at the closed door. She reached to the shelving that flanked the door and picked up her Glock, wondering for a moment how normal people answered the door at ten o'clock at night.

She peered through the security peephole but saw nothing. Daisy's barking evolved into a steady string of growls, making it impossible to hear any sounds coming from the hallway. She wiped the perspiration that had formed on her hand before unlocking the latch and pulling the door open.

There was no one there. Mia felt the staccato pounding heartbeat in her throat begin to ease. She took a step into the hall and looked both ways. Daisy's growls escalated and Mia snapped her head back to find the little dog threatening a package on Mia's doormat.

A package that was bleeding.

8

The package held two dolls—identical in every way —and naked, drenched in what looked like blood. Mia didn't have time to drop it off at a lab to see for sure— or the time to wait the three weeks necessary for getting an answer back. Nor did she want to alert Jack to the fact that the nasty thing had been delivered to her. It was enough that the message had been sent and received.

The question of *who* sent it vibrated through Mia the rest of the night and into the morning. She wrapped the grisly package and stashed it in the top shelf of her closet, then showered and changed the sheets in Jack's room. She slept fitfully, the little dog beside her, until Jack came into the room and slipped into bed with her, drawing her close to him, and, after a murmured *I love you* fell asleep immediately.

She woke to the sounds of vomiting in the adjoining bathroom.

"Jack?" Mia ran to the bathroom door and laid her cheek against it.

"I'm fine," he rasped. "Didn't get my flu shot. Just the cherry on my crap week." He opened the door and smiled wanly at her. His hair was tousled and even in the dim morning light, he looked pale.

"You're sick," Mia said. "Go back to bed."

"On my way. Afraid our makeup sex will have to wait."

"Oh, you're not off the hook for that, my friend," Mia said, pulling him back to bed and pushing him onto it.

"Very funny," he groaned.

"What can I get you? Toast? Tea?"

"Nothing. I'm sorry, Mia."

"Don't be ridiculous," she said, tucking the covers around him. "Just feel better. Will Daisy bother you if I let her stay?"

He shook his head, his eyes already closed. Mia hesitated to kiss him. No sense in both of them getting sick.

As she drove to Lawrenceville, Mia's mind was abuzz with everything that had happened in the last few hours. While she hated that Jack was sick, a small part of her was glad he'd be out of action for a bit. She could put his case—and what did or didn't happen and whose fault that was—on the back burner for long enough to get some traction on her own case.

And first and foremost with that was who the hell sent her the bloody, naked dolls? If it was a warning to her, did that mean she was getting close? Of her four suspects—Cook, Derek, Cargill and Turner—only Cook was in the clear. And something about Turner made her believe the gesture was a little too crass for him. But was it believable that portly Barry Cargill would come huffing and puffing up Mia's stairs to leave the package? To what end? He'd been extremely upset to know Mia was reopening the possibility that someone else besides Cook had killed Victoria, but this effort seemed way too energetic for him.

That left Derek. But what lowlife would send naked dolls representing his own sisters? That was taking twisted to a whole new level.

Mia crested Spaghetti Junction, heading northeast toward Lawrenceville, thirty-five miles from Atlanta. She left I-85 at Gwinnett Place Mall and exited onto University Parkway, which took her into the heart of the town. On her list today was a couple who had used Victoria to babysit their kids years ago. Unfortunately, Rhonda Kilpatrick had called the police after Mia's visit to request no one else bother her family again. The police notified Peterson, who'd emailed the message to Mia the previous afternoon.

She knew, technically, that trying to talk to the twins again could get her in major trouble—*if she were caught*—but she also knew she wasn't done with them. They were the treasure trove—even beyond Victoria's diary—that would help Mia find out what was going on with Victoria beyond the scam.

Checking her GPS, Mia quickly found the address she was looking for. It was a small town after all. Debbie and Robert Olds had lived next door to Victoria's family for fifteen years. While Mia had neglected to mention to Mrs. Olds when she called yesterday that she was interviewing them on behalf of the sexual pervert in custody for Victoria's death, she didn't feel guilty about it.

It all comes down to nailing the guy who killed Victoria. We're on the same team. I'm just playing on a different field.

Victoria's old neighborhood was blue-collar, but tidy. The homes were built at least forty years ago and the landscaping was mature and lush. Mia parked her car at the front curb in front of the Olds' house and checked her watch. She was early.

Debbie Olds opened the front door before Mia cleared the first step on the porch. She was extremely fat, so much so that her arms stuck out as if they were too small for her body. An image of a T-Rex came unbidden to Mia's mind. Mrs. Olds smiled broadly and gestured for Mia to enter.

"Hello, Mrs. Olds," Mia said, stepping inside. The smell of bacon and fried food seemed to waft visibly in the air around her and for a moment Mia's stomach twisted.

"Come in, come in, darlin,'" Mrs. Olds said. "Bob will be out shortly. I've got tea out on the back deck. It's warm enough, don't you think?"

"Yes, it's lovely," Mia said, her eyes darting to the dark interior of the living room as they passed. She saw a drab collection of old furniture; it looked like it hadn't been updated since the couple first moved in.

"I know you want to hear all about Vickie," Mrs. Olds said. "My goodness, I can't tell you how upset the whole town was to hear about everything she had gotten up to. We certainly never knew. That wasn't our Vickie."

Unspoken message: that's what comes from moving to Atlanta.

The deck overlooked a small backyard bordered on three sides by a thick wood. It was just warm enough to see a few dogwood trees starting to blossom—the advent of the famous Atlanta spring. Mia saw a few of the telltale flowering trees tucked away in the deepest part of the backyard woods.

"It's beautiful," she said as she sat on a hard wooden chair.

"Thank you," Debbie Olds said. "I hope you like your tea sweet."

"Of course," Mia said. Nothing got you labeled a Yankee faster than asking for unsweetened iced tea. "Again, let me thank you for seeing me on such short notice."

"Child, Bob and I don't have anything else to do. You could've called up an hour ago and we'd still be sitting right here like we are now."

"Well, I'm grateful. Do you mind my asking some questions now?"

"Fire away. Will the story be running in the Atlanta Journal? If it does, I know the Lawrenceville paper will pick it up. They've run a lot on Vickie the last three months but I'd like to see something that doesn't paint our girl as a trollop. You know what I mean?"

"Yes, I do," Mia said, reminding herself that she never told the Olds that she was a journalist. Was it her fault that that's the first conclusion they jumped to?

"You knew Victoria when her family lived next door," Mia prodded.

"Fifteen years they lived there. And Vickie, of course, too."

"What happened to them? They moved away?"

Debbie Olds hesitated and then broke into a smile as her husband opened the door from the kitchen and entered onto the deck.

"Here's my Bob," she said. "This nice young lady was just asking why the Baskervilles moved away," she said to him.

Robert Olds was the physical opposite of his heavyset wife, with loose jowls and flaccid skin in his face that gave him a bloodhound look, also a perennially unhappy expression. Mia wondered if it was even possible for the man to smile with all that flesh dragging downward against his chin.

"Mark Baskerville left as soon as they moved in," he said as he seated himself across from Mia in a rocking chair.

"Oh, that's right, he did," Debbie said. She turned to Mia. "We never really knew him. It was Vickie's mother who bought the house. She worked down at the elementary school as the school nurse. Although I don't think she was real nurse. In those days, just having a good head on your shoulders could get you a job as a school nurse."

"I see," Mia said. "And did Victoria have brothers and sisters?" Mia knew the answer but was hoping to get the pair talking about Victoria's family life without having to lead them too much.

"No, it was just Vickie and her mom, Slyvie," Debbie said.

"How old was Vickie when they moved in?"

"About ten?" She turned to her husband who confirmed with a nod.

"And she babysat y'all's kids?"

"Well, not right away," Debbie said with a laugh. "What kind of a babysitter would be ten years old?"

"But she wasn't much older than that," Bob said, frowning at his wife.

"But she *was* older," Debbie said firmly.

"Your kids have all flown the nest, I guess?"

"Oh my, yes. Our oldest girl is married with two little ones of her own. Lives in Dacula. Our boy is twenty and has a very good job at the Gwinnett Mall."

Mia tapped her pen against her notepad. This was going to be delicate, and she hated to start asking the questions that were going to wipe the welcoming smiles off their faces, but she was here to get information she couldn't read in Victoria's file. And for that, she needed to push the edge a little.

"So, I suppose your family knows the Kilpatricks?"

Sure enough, at the mention of the twins the pair stiffened in unison.

"Rhonda Kilpatrick is an unfortunate creature," Debbie said, clasping her hands in her lap as if her proclamation was all that needed to be said on the subject.

"Unfortunate in that she was too loose with her kids?" Mia prompted.

Debbie caught the eye of her husband and he seemed to wake up.

"The Kilpatricks are not our kind of people," he said. "Rhonda's boy was constantly in trouble and, well, the twins have been in the paper for three months now as I reckon you already know."

"She wasn't trying to suggest that Vickie ever wanted to get Andy and Bryanna involved in anything like that," Debbie said. But she looked at Mia when she said it and she didn't smile.

"Of course not," Bob said. "Our two have a hell of a lot more sense than that."

"Plus, they were raised right," Debbie said. "Church every Sunday. After-school sports. And a strong sense of duty to family and country."

"I heard a rumor that Victoria and Derek used to date," Mia said. "Is that true?"

"That's a good question" Debbie said, clearly happy she had somehow slipped off the hot seat in place of Derek. "I don't know how long they were together but I'm sure it was always more in Derek's head. I'm not even absolutely positive it's true."

"Was there anybody else special in her life growing up?"

"Well, of course there was Drew."

Bingo. The mysterious D.

"Her boyfriend?"

"All through school. The two of them were hotter than a jalapeño while it lasted. It was heartbreaking how it ended. Even you have to agree to that," she said to her husband, who shrugged.

"What happened?"

"Vickie got caught, you know, with a baby. We went to the same church, did I mention that?"

Mia shook her head.

"She wanted to keep it, and now that I see how things turned out I'm not sorry she didn't, but at the time she was devastated."

"How?"

"Drew's mama didn't like Vickie. *At all.* When she found out Vickie was PG, Alice did everything in her power to keep the two apart. Drew's weak. I'll say that and it's the only positive thing I can think to say about him. He did listen to his mama."

"A lot of good it did him," her husband said.

So Alice was Victoria's ex-boyfriend's mother.

"What happened?"

"Drew broke up with her. And broke her heart in the process. Our pastor convinced her that the best thing for the baby—and for her too—would be to give it up. Vickie knew what it was like not to have a daddy."

"Tell her the rest of the story," Bob said gruffly.

Debbie frowned and then her brow cleared. "Oh!" she said. "Six months after the baby was born, Drew went away for felony murder. Twenty years to life."

Mia whistled. "That's steep."

"The manager of the convenience store died during the robbery."

Mia tried to imagine the kind of life Victoria had come from—losing her father, her first love, her baby. She already knew from the file Peterson gave her that her grades were good enough to qualify for the state scholarship. The University of Georgia wasn't twenty miles away and it was a good state school. But there was no record of her having even applied to it.

"You never said why Victoria and her family moved away," Mia said.

"Oh, that was sad, too. Poor Slyvie got breast cancer. Vickie nursed her until she died, then graduated high school and sold the house without a backward glance, didn't she, Bob?"

Bob didn't answer.

"And moved to Atlanta?"

"We never knew where she'd gone off to. It wasn't until the papers started printing pictures of her that we even knew the Internet Hussy was our Vickie."

"Let me ask you, Drew's mother's name was Alice?"

"That's right. Alice Smith."

"Is she still around?"

"We see her at church now and then. She's not in regular attendance if you know what I mean. What with all this happening to Vickie, she's certainly been louder than ever."

"She still hates Victoria after all these years?"

"She surely does. Even though Vickie and Drew broke up months before he tried to knock off the Jiffy Mart, Alice always blamed Vickie for Drew's going to prison. It didn't make any sense."

"But then love doesn't," Bob said.

By the time Mia walked away from the front steps away from the Olds' home, it was already late afternoon and she'd had no fewer than four text messages from Jack asking when she was coming home.

She smiled ruefully at the texts. Even the biggest tough guys turn into babies when they're sick. She headed back to Atlanta and punched in her mother's number for the long ride home.

"Well, I wondered when I might hear from you," Jessie answered.

"Sorry. Been busy."

"Bill said you had a new and very high profile case."

"Yeah. And I think I'm just starting to get some headway with it. What's new on your end? Got the cake and the catering all scheduled?"

"The cake, yes, the catering, not yet. Oh! I talked with Jack this afternoon. He's going to do the rehearsal dinner."

"Cool."

"And I talked with Cindy, Bill's ex-wife."

"She's about three exes back, isn't she?"

"Two, but she is the mother of his children."

"Okay, well what did she have to say?"

"She was very nice. Wished me every happiness."

"She's not invited, is she?"

"We're still discussing it."

"Don't tell me. You're in favor and the chief is a nay vote."

Jessie sighed heavily. "He has a lot on his plate right now."

"By that you mean a one hundred and twenty pound pain in the ass by the name of Mindy."

"She's going to be family in about ninety days, Mia."

"If you say so. To change the subject, how did Jack sound when you talked to him?"

"Very ill. What is it, food poisoning?"

Mia laughed. "Don't even *breathe* that word around a professional chef, Mom. No, he thinks it's the flu."

"What's going on with his case?"

"Seems Jack's lawyer wants to delay the prelim and Jack wants to waive his right to a speedy trial."

"That doesn't sound good."

"I know, right?"

"Bill said the ME and the detectives at the scene will testify at the preliminary hearing. He said the prosecution might call you, too, Mia. You need to be prepared."

Mia felt her good mood deflate. How was she going to pretend that none of this happened with Jack if she had to stand up in court and lie under oath?

"What in the world can I say?"

"The truth, of course."

"Even if the truth sends Jack to prison?"

"If Jack goes to prison, dear girl, it will be his *actions* that sent him there, not your testimony."

"That sounds pretty, Mom, but it's not true and you know it."

*****

Maxwell shifted uncomfortably in his chair. God knows he should have done this years ago; sat the girl down and talked to her straight. She was always an alien being, her head in her computer. And he had always been a people person. Could there be a father and daughter more different?

"Hey, Dad." Mindy swept into the sushi restaurant and gave him a kiss before taking her seat opposite him. He was amazed at how much she looked like his mother in her younger days. But whereas his mother looked mousey, Mindy took the same brown hair, pale complexion and narrow green eyes and brought an intensity and power to the whole package that always startled him.

Not pretty, exactly, but arresting. Definitely arresting.

"Mindy," he said, smiling at her. "You look comfortable."

Now, why did he say that? She was dressed in jeans and a floppy tunic of some kind. She didn't exactly look like a homeless person, just not like she was meeting someone for lunch downtown. He watched her flinch and he could've kicked himself.

"Yes, well, thank you, Dad," she said, picking up the menu and gazing at it. "That was, after all my goal, to appear comfortable."

"I didn't mean it like that."

"It doesn't matter. So what will you have? I know you have trouble in places like this."

"I'll have whatever you have."

He'd already grabbed a sandwich earlier. Mindy knew he didn't eat this crap; probably was the reason she chose the restaurant. He could play her game if he needed to. Just stay cool, keep everything nice and pleasant.

Mindy slapped down her menu when the waiter came over and ordered raw tuna for both of them. Maxwell was certain she picked the most disgusting thing on the menu just to rattle him. He wouldn't let that happen.

"So," he said, after the waiter walked away, "I talked with Jess and she really wants you in the wedding as a bridesmaid, with Mia."

"That's so sweet," Mindy said, but her face didn't reflect her words. "She sent me a *welcome to the family* note the other day."

"Did she? Well, that's Jess for you. I'm glad."

"You must have told her about my wild days before I settled down and got married, Dad," Mindy said, her eyes glassy with excitement. Maxwell automatically stiffened in preparation for whatever she had up her sleeve.

"I haven't told her anything negative about you," he said, eyeing her carefully.

"Oh, no? Well, she offered to help me score weed if I didn't have my own source so I just assumed you'd talked to her."

Maxwell's gut churned. "I don't believe you." *What was wrong with this girl? What had always been wrong with her?*

"I can show you her note if you like," Mindy said, her eyes round and eager to help. She pulled a notecard out of her purse. Even from across the table, he recognized it as one of Jess's.

"Dear Mindy," Mindy read. "Thank you so much for calling me the other day." She looked up. "I called her last week to say hi. I'm surprised she didn't mention it to you."

He held out his hand for the note and she passed it to him.

Dear Mindy, Thank you so much for calling the other day. If you need a source for what we were talking about (hint hint, rhymes with pot) let me know. I'm still in the game for at least the cost of my mortgage every month. I hope we find an opportunity soon to get together. Best wishes, Jess Kazmaroff.

"Do you recognize her handwriting?"

For a moment, he wasn't sure he wasn't going to throw up the sandwich he'd bolted the hour earlier. He stared at the notecard, uncomprehending, unbelieving.

"I have to ask, Dad, how much do you really know about her?"

"Stop it, Mindy." He still couldn't stop looking at the card. It looked just like Jess's handwriting. Would his crazy daughter really have forged it?

"Did you know she had an arrest for pot?" Mindy asked, taking chopsticks out of the paper sleeve in front of her.

"Back in the sixties," he said, placing the notecard on the table. "Everybody did."

"*You* didn't. *Mom* didn't. How about the more recent charge? For resisting arrest? Do you know about that one?"

"That a was a peaceful protest. Jess and fifty other people were hauled in on an Occupy Wall Street demonstration."

How did Mindy know about all this shit? Of course. She'd have gone online to check Jess out. That was a given.

"Oh, good. How about the prostitution arrest? I know you haven't bothered to check the public court records on your intended but, honestly, Dad, you might want to."

He didn't want to ask, didn't want her to know she'd gotten to him. But he had to know.

"What are you talking about?"

"It was ten years ago, so maybe it doesn't matter to you since it was so long ago, but she was arrested on charges of prostitution. Frankly, I didn't know you were so cool, Dad."

Could this be true? Is there a way in hell it could be true? Jess was a bit of a wild card. Why hadn't Jess told him that Mindy called? He touched the note again, working to push the word *prostitution* to the back of his mind.

He glanced at Mindy. Her eyes positively danced like he hadn't seen since he'd bought Mindy her first laptop. What kind of strange creature was this child of his? To delight in uncovering and delivering such poison? To possibly have even created it herself?

"Gee, Dad," Mindy said, smiling broadly, "you look a little queasy around the gills. Trust me, the tuna isn't bad here. They almost never come with parasites anymore."

*****

Jack surveyed the living room with a critical eye. He'd removed all the tissue boxes, throat lozenge papers and assorted tea mugs from the coffee table—everything that served as evidence of his extremely nonproductive day while Mia was gone. Not that she expected him to do any work when he was sick. He showered and dressed, glancing again at his phone to see she hadn't checked in since the last time she'd texted *on my way* an hour ago. He'd slept for five hours —until just after lunch and awakened refreshed if still weak.

The fact was, he really had needed a reason to slow down and rest. What he *didn't* need was think about Jim Martin—who he was, who his family was. If there was any way Jack could just zero in on that amazing girl driving home at this very moment who would soon be in his arms then maybe he could stop himself from thinking about how selfish it was to allow her to put her life on hold for him if he did have to…go away for a time.

Determined not to let her bring up his case, but not to deflect it too harshly either, Jack poured himself another mug of hot tea just as his phone rang. It was his lawyer.

"Bad news."

Shit. Defense attorneys should be legally prevented from starting any phone conversation with those two words.

"What?"

"Just floated the possibility of a deal in the courthouse hallway today and it's probably not going to be one you'll be excited to take."

"Fine. I'm going with a not guilty plea anyway. As you know."

"Yeah, but that's not the bad news."

"Do you mind spitting it out?"

"I heard it from someone who knows someone that if they decide there's probable cause at the hearing, they're going to revoke bail. Sorry, Jack. If they charge you formally at the preliminary, they'll take you into custody."

*****

The rain always seemed louder from Jack's room. His bedroom window faced the parking lot. Maybe all that asphalt made the difference in creating a drumming effect that was lost among the trees and bushes that flanked the guestroom where Mia usually slept.

While Jack strongly suggested she sleep in her own bed tonight to prevent her catching what he had, she insisted on sleeping together. Even if it meant getting sick, it was better than being estranged for one more night.

The minute she walked into the condo, she knew something was "off"—and not just because he was sick. He smiled and asked questions about her case but she could tell there was something missing behind his eyes. She'd promised herself she wouldn't ask about his case unless he volunteered it. And he didn't.

Mutually deciding that tonight was as good a time as any to have a completely stress-free, hot-button free evening, they curled up on the couch together and watched TV until they both nodded off. Once in the bedroom, Jack was asleep within minutes and for that Mia was grateful. He needed the rest.

She watched him sleep for a moment, his face finally relaxed, and then slipped out of bed and went to the living room. There, she pulled out her laptop and the printout Nathan Turner had given her of the men Victoria had *not* met up with. Using Victoria's password, Mia logged onto Victoria's profile and went to her history on *Atlanta Loves*. Matching the list of men in Victoria's site history with the sheet that Turner had given her, Mia clicked on each name and read the exchanged messages.

There were hundreds and hundreds of names.

Even so, things went relatively quickly. It was clear after the first few exchanges that Victoria was fishing for a certain kind of man—one interested in sex out of the ordinary, although she couched it in less subtle terms. Mia read one exchange:

<Hi, Sid. Thank you for being interested in my profile. I was very intrigued by yours, too. Have you had much luck with *Atlanta Loves*?>

<Hey, beautiful. I got lucky the second I found you. Care to meet for a drink?>

<That sounds good. I should warn you, I have very exotic tastes.>

<Are we still talking alcohol?>

<Ha ha. Maybe not. Does that scare you?>

<I'm a hard man to scare.>

<Ooh. I like my men hard.>

A few days had passed with no communication, and then Victoria reached out again.

<Sid? You still interested in getting together? Let me know.">

There were no more email messages between them. Victoria's responses were clearly designed to weed out the men looking for a possible love partner. Sometimes the exchanges ended after Victoria's first response, sometimes they went on a little longer. The police had access to the exchanges that had actually led to a face-to-face.

Mia glanced at the clock. It was after two in the morning. She wasn't sure what this exercise was showing her, she just knew it was a road the cops hadn't gone down. She ran a finger down the long columns in the ten-page document and found six men whose addresses were not included. She frowned and decided to start with them first since they'd be the trickiest to locate.

Going back to *Atlanta Loves*, she clicked on the first name, Ben Mattherson, and worked her way down. An hour later, just about to go back to bed, she clicked on the fifth name with no address, a Jeffrey Wojinziky. Reading the exchange between him and Victoria, Mia found herself waking up. A tingling sensation crept up her bare arms.

<Hello, Jeff. Mind if I call you Jeff?>

<Sure. And you go by Victoria?>

<I do.>

<That's a beautiful name. I'd love to meet you in person.>

<That can be arranged. What did you have in mind?>

Mia frowned when she saw the date on the next entry. For whatever reason, a couple of weeks had passed before Jeff responded again to Victoria.

<Sorry about that. Where were we?>

<You were trying to decide if I was too hot to handle.>

<I think I already know the answer to that.>

<Funny guy. I'd love to see you try.>

<Just tell me when and where.>

<How about the parking lot of The Gold Club?>

Mia recognized the name of the infamous Midtown strip club Victoria referenced. She was doing her damnedest to find out if Jeff was open to the kinky stuff.

<I'm game if you are>

<Thursday at ten o'clock?>

Holy shit! They were setting up a meeting, and because they weren't swapping numbers the dating site's data scan bots hadn't picked up on it.

Mia felt a rush of adrenaline. She had a suspect the cops didn't know about, one *who'd met Victoria in person.*

That was the end of their messages. Obviously, they'd met up and found other ways of contacting each other.

Was this J?

It was the first solid lead that hadn't been discovered by the cops. Mia examined Jeff Wojinziky's profile picture. He had a pleasant face, ginger-hair and a light beard. His background info said he was a plumber who loves the Georgia Bulldogs. No college listed. No employer listed. Mia tapped a pencil against her bottom lip trying to put together the blue-collar plumber with the enigmatic Victoria.

An email notice appeared in the upper right hand of her screen and she clicked on it. It wasn't unusual to get emails in the middle of the night, and when she saw that it was from her client, George Peterson, she was even less surprised. Lawyers worked long and late.

Hello, Ms. Kazmaroff,

It's been a busy day but I couldn't end it without notifying you that your services will no longer be needed in the case of Joshua Cook vs. the State, as Mr. Cook was cleared of all charges and released from police custody late this afternoon.

Please stop working on Mr. Cook's behalf immediately as, with his release, this is once more an open police investigation.

Thank you for your help. If you would be so kind as to invoice me for the balance of your time, I would me most grateful.

Kindest regards,

George Peterson.

Mia stared at the email. She reread it three times, but no matter how many times she read it the message didn't change.

She was fired.

And Joshua Cook was a free man.

9

Chief William Maxwell stood in the side yard of Jess's house and threaded a long green hose along the ground. It had been years since he'd done yard work. Jess had a lawn guy but there was always work to do.

The sound of the screen door slamming made him look toward the house. He wasn't surprised to see Mia pulling on her jacket and jogging across the lawn toward him. He'd watched her and Jack drive up a few minutes ago.

They were supposed to be here to discuss the menu for the rehearsal dinner that Jack was catering, but with that lowlife Cook cleared on the Internet Hussy case he knew the real point of the visit.

"Morning, Chief," she called to him. "Thinking of lighting a match to it?"

"Mia," he said, nodding in greeting.

"Interesting news about Cook. How'd he slip the noose?"

Maxwell squinted at the sun dipping behind the sourwoods in Jessie's front yard. He couldn't help looking for signs of a pot garden and he hated himself for even thinking of it. A quick check into the police records ten years back popped up the prostitution charge just as Mindy said. Naturally, she'd failed to mention that the charge was in connection to a series of mass arrests at a political rally involving better wages and healthcare for sex workers and that the charge had been dropped.

The handwritten pot note was a little harder to explain. Was it genuine? Could it possibly be?

"Chief?"

He turned and looked at Mia.

"You were about to tell me how Cook went free," she said. "Are you okay?"

"I'm fine. Someone came forward with a time-stamp video of a party Cook was at during the time of the murder."

"They were able to pinpoint time of death that narrowly?"

"Narrowly enough for Cook."

"And you guys have nobody else that looks good? What about Barry Cargill? Are you looking at him next? Oh! And I've been meaning to ask you about Derek Kilpatrick's alibi."

"I'm not talking about the case with you, Mia."

"Why not? I don't work for Bentley & Jamison anymore."

"You know the case is reopened, right?"

"Of course."

"That means you need to surrender all your files and you don't go near anybody you've been questioning up to now." He glanced at her to see if she could tell he was bluffing. If she wanted to be difficult, he'd have to get a warrant for the files.

And Mia was always difficult.

"Did you hear me, Mia?"

She walked over to the hose and stretched out a kink in it. "Maybe some things I found out could be helpful to the police."

"Type them up and include them with the files you have."

"Sounds like a brush off, Chief."

"Is that your mother calling us?" He turned to head back to the house and Mia grabbed his arm.

"Chief, I'd really like to be kept in the loop on this. Please."

Maxwell tucked Mia's hand on his arm as if he were the father of the bride escorting her down the aisle and patted her hand. He couldn't help but see the similarities between Mia and Mindy. Both were hardheaded and passionate. Both saw only their side of the equation. He'd failed Mindy, that was clear. In a thousand different ways. He knew that was a mess and he knew it was his fault.

"That's not going to be possible, darlin'," he said brightly. "But what *is* possible is the clear and irrefutable evidence of maple bacon and waffles I smell coming from the house. Shall we?"

The last thing Maxwell wanted to do was ask Jess about the stupid note—especially after he'd told her to ignore Mindy's troublemaking. His mood sank lower with every footstep he took toward the house and the woman he loved more than anything else in the world.

*****

Mia looked at Jack as she drove them back to Atlantic Station from her mother's house. He still looked weak. He'd spoken very little at Jess's. Not himself at all.

Almost as if he thought he might not be available for Mom's big day.

"What did the chief say to you when you were outside?" he asked.

"Basically told me to butt out."

"Well, that's not a surprise."

"I know things, Jack," Mia said hotly. "I can be a help. Maxwell is always talking about how the department doesn't have enough money or resources and here I am—a walking, talking resource ready to be used in any way necessary."

"Please don't lead with your chin like that until I'm feeling better," he said, a faint smile on his lips.

"You look awful."

"Thanks. I feel pretty crappy."

"Don't you think you should have your lawyer push the prelim back? You're sick, Jack."

She hadn't meant to be the first one to bring it up, but there were limits to her powers of self-control.

"How I feel is irrelevant for what's going down on Tuesday," he said softly.

"What?" She snapped her head to look at him. "Do you know something?"

"Not really. Just…" He lifted a hand as if to explain something to her and then dropped it. "Not really."

"You need to be in bed."

"Again with the sex talk when I'm in no condition to do anything about it." He closed his eyes and leaned his head against the window.

An hour later, Jack was tucked in bed and asleep. Mia sat on the couch in the living room and tried to process everything that had happened.

Cook was free—not even on the hook for trying to buy underage sex since the twins were not, after all, underage. It was all so frustrating. When she tried to log onto Victoria's *Atlanta Love's* site, the password didn't work anymore. To hear Maxwell complain about the Atlanta Police IT Department, she would've expected them to take a lot longer before closing down that portal.

Figures this would be the one time they rise to the occasion.

And where does that leave everything else? Derek? Cargill? If Cook really is innocent then the killer was out there walking around free. Mia ran her fingers through Daisy's topknot and tried to think of what she could do if the police really did close all avenues on the case. She glanced around the room and noticed Jack's smartphone on the coffee table.

He must be sick. He normally isn't five inches from that thing.

She had it in her hand and open before she even knew she was doing it. It wasn't password protected. *Trying to ignore a creeping sense of guilt,* she went straight to his email addresses, found his lawyer's name and opened the most recent one. She drilled down into the history and read every exchange between them since the arrest, then closed it and set it back on the coffee table.

Jack was going to plead not guilty in three days' time. And then he was going to be taken into custody to await trial. Mia looked in the direction of the bedroom and felt a terrible weight press on her shoulders. He was going down this terrible road alone.

The man was stubborn and he was strong.

Even Mia knew that was a deadly combination.

The next morning, Jack was much improved. Mia could see he would be healthy enough to take the stand in his own defense. She could also see that if somebody didn't get off her butt and do something, soon, he would be well enough to be led out of the courtroom in leg manacles too.

She showered and dressed, walked the dog and came into the living room, where Jack rested on the couch.

"You look better," she said.

"Liar."

"I have to go do that bridesmaid thing."

"I'll be fine, Mia. Go."

"I won't be long."

"I'll probably be asleep the whole time you're gone. Don't hurry."

Truth was, she hated to leave him—especially since she couldn't get past the feeling that these might be the last few days she had with him where they weren't separated by bars. But she couldn't let him know that. He was obviously determined to do this without her involvement.

The drive to the wedding dress boutique was a short one, but filled with thoughts of Cook and then of Jack in a confusing Ping-Pong match of images and thoughts.

Jess had insisted Mia meet Mindy at the shop since they were the only two bridesmaids and needed to coordinate their outfits. Mia was fairly sure all she really needed to coordinate was buying the same dress that Mindy did, but clearly Jess was hoping to foster a detente between the soon-to-be stepsisters.

She arrived early at the bridal shop and handed the paper with the catalog number and her size written on it to the sales girl. She'd seen a photo of the dress at her mother's house and it didn't look too bad. Mia rarely wore dresses so she didn't expect to get much use out of it beyond the wedding day, but it didn't matter. She'd wear a duck costume if that's what her mother needed from her.

"The Princess scoop neck in cocoa chiffon," the sales girl said as she came back to Mia, the dress draped in light transparent layers over one arm. "Follow me to the dressing room, please."

Mia fell into step, took the dress and deposited on the floor of the room her jeans, ankle motorcycle boots and sweatshirt that she meant to launder after her last trip to the barn. She was long-waisted, with long legs— a surprising combination on a petite frame—and one that almost always made her feel like a miniature Barbie doll. When the dress smoothed over her hips in its froth of chiffon, even Mia had to admit she looked ready for a fairy tale.

"How does it fit?" the sales girl called to her from outside the room.

Mia stepped out and in front of the three-way mirror. "Good, I think," she said.

"It's perfect with your skin color," the girl said, frowning as if to belie her words. "You have a lot of olive in your skin. Very nice. Makes you glow."

Mia pinked up at the compliment and turned to look at herself from the back. Would Jack get a chance to see her in this dress? Her shoulders sagged at the thought. How can she be trying on dresses and feeling pretty when he was back home wondering if he was going to prison?

"Yes, it's nice," Mia said. "I'll take it." She went back to the dressing room and carefully transferred the dress back to its hanger. When she came out, the girl took the dress away and Mia followed her to the cash register.

Mindy still hadn't shown up and a clawing finger of doubt pinched at Mia. Would she not come? Would she refuse to wear a bridesmaid's dress at Jess's wedding? As she approached the cash register, Mia saw a woman in line ahead of her. The sales girl gave Mia an apologetic look but Mia didn't mind waiting.

The woman in front of Mia was on her cell phone and drumming long, lacquered nails against the counter as she spoke. It was interesting to Mia that someone could be so clueless that they were holding everyone else up—unless they knew they were and just didn't care? Mia leaned against the counter to wait.

"Yes, well, I heard he just croaked and nobody even knew he had a heart condition. What heart condition? That's what I said."

The woman spoke loudly in a brash New Jersey accent. The sales woman who was waiting on her had stopped ringing up her purchase and held out the woman's credit card as if she had a question about it.

Oh, this should be good. Mia smiled. *Better than Saturday morning TV.*

"I told you that already," the woman brayed on the phone. "Supposedly he had some kind of pills and as long as he took them, no problem. What? What is it?" The woman shifted her phone to another ear but was now clearly talking to the saleswoman.

"It was declined, I'm afraid," the woman said.

"Impossible. Try it again."

"I've already run it through twice."

"Well, run it through three times. That card is good. Eleanor, I'm going to have to call you back. This moron at the bridal shop doesn't know how to run a credit card machine."

Mia watched the saleswoman's impassive face. Clearly, in her business, she'd been called worse.

A few minutes later, as Mia left the shop with her own dress, bagged and draped over her arm, she scanned the parking lot for the chief's daughter but was secretly grateful not to see her. As she hung up the dress in the back of her car, a thought came to her.

At first it was unformed and negligible, really nothing more than a feeling. But as she secured her seatbelt, Mia caught sight of the New Jersey woman in the parking lot getting into her car—and the thought burst into her brain fully formed.

Was it possible? Was it at all probable? Maybe if you believed just for a moment that Jack's guy really did just—what was it the woman said?—croak? Then maybe, just maybe...

Mia pulled her tablet from the glove compartment and opened an Internet browser, typing *can you drop dead of heart condition?* in the search window. Within minutes, she was toggling between three websites that listed several heart ailments that, left untreated, could result in an abrupt death.

A long shot. A Hail Mary play. A one-in-a-million chance.

With trembling fingers, Mia opened her smartphone and scrolled through her photographs until she came to the one she'd taken of the file folder Jack had left out when he didn't think she was paying attention. It was the file on the man who died that night at the fire extinguisher plant. He was forty-two years old. Mia felt her pulse quicken.

She isolated his address and plugged it into her GPS system.

It wasn't much but it was better than nothing. And in Mia's brief experience, a wild leap of faith, a little guts and a whole lot of nothing had solved some pretty big-ass cases.

10

"Let me do the talking, okay?" Mindy flicked a hair off her mother's shoulder as they stood on Jess Kazmaroff's doorstep.

"Of course, dear. Have you met her? Is she pretty?" Cindy Maxwell stood next to her daughter, staring at the door as if addressing it. There was a light scent of alcohol about her. Not surprising. This wasn't an easy errand and Mindy was mildly impressed that her mother was able to come at all. If necessary, Mindy could have done it alone. Just not as convincingly.

When the door opened, she enjoyed the startled reaction their visit caused in Jess.

"Well, hello," Jess said, looking from Mindy to her mother. "What a surprise. I thought you were…" She looked at Mindy and smiled tremulously. "Weren't you and Mia meeting at the bridal shop today?"

"Oh, crap, was that today? I totally forgot," Mindy said. "Can we talk to you?"

"Yes, of course," Jess said, backing up and holding the door open for them. Mindy had to give her mother a nudge to get her moving across the threshold.

"We have a little problem and when my mother and I got to talking about it…oh, have you two met?"

She had to hand it to Jess, her smile looked as genuine and open as if she really meant it. She shook Mindy's mother's hand.

"We haven't," Jess said. "But I'm so glad to finally meet you."

Wisely, Jess made no mention of how much the chief had or hadn't said about his ex-wife. Probably better that way. Jess was fast on her feet. Mindy had to give her that.

"You, too," Cindy Maxwell murmured. Mindy had practically dressed her mother that morning and it had been no easy task. After the divorce, Cindy had taken to wearing yoga pants and sweatshirts and her diet had altered in order to more comfortably fill them. Now she was overweight—which was unusual for an alcoholic, but that was her mother, always defying the odds and coming out on the less positive side of the statistics.

"I know this is probably indelicate," Mindy said, looking around the living room and trying to imagine her dad lounging on the couch or fiddling with the TV, "but we need to ask you something about the wedding. And we'd just as soon my dad not know."

"I see," Jess said. "Can I get you a coffee? I just made a pot."

"That would be awesome, Jess," Mindy said. "Wouldn't it, Mom?"

Cindy nodded her head and Mindy gave her another small push, this time in the direction of the kitchen where Jess was walking. Over her shoulder, Mindy saw what she was looking for in a darkened corner of the living room.

The three walked into the kitchen and Mindy promptly sat at the round dining table hoping her mother would take her lead. She did. They watched Jess as she pulled two mugs out of the cabinet over the sink, poured the coffees and returned to the table.

"How do you take your coffee?"

Before her mother could speak, Mindy said, "Oh, with everything you've got. Cream, sugar, the works."

She pressed a foot down firmly on her mother's toe and was rewarded with a startled look on Cindy's face. Jess turned to fetch the cream and sugar, as well as spoons, napkins, and a pound cake she had on the counter.

"You said it was indelicate?" Jess said.

"Somewhat," Mindy said. "Although I'm sure we can work it out. Mom, can you start? I need to run to the bathroom."

"Across the living room, first door on the left," Jess said, as she brought the cake and a large cutting knife to the table. Mindy saw her turn quizzically to Cindy. "You have my curiosity," she said, still smiling.

Mindy moved into the living room and walked past the couch to the other side of the room before turning and silently retracing her steps. She could hear her mother's high-pitched voice begin to recite the script Mindy had gone over with her on the way to Jess's house.

Cindy spoke slowly, as if unsure of what she was saying—as well she might be—but without taking a breath or adding any natural inflections. Normally, her mother's speech pattern got solidly on Mindy's last nerve but today she thanked God for it. The more agitated Cindy got—as surely today's topic would generate without any problem—the more incoherent she would become. Exactly as planned.

Jess's computer, like a lot of people's, was set up in the living room. It was a PC that appeared to be several years old. In the course of idle chit-chat with her dad—*only it's never really idle, is it?*—Mindy discovered that Jess was nervous about using the Internet. Her daughter, Mia, had set up the computer for her, but if the thin layer of dust on the keyboard was any indication it was rarely used.

Which suited Mindy perfectly.

She booted the machine up and quickly typed in one of five possible passwords in the search space. She hit gold with the third one—*Daisy*. To hear her father rabbit on about that stupid dog, you'd think it was already listed in his will. She jammed a thumb drive into the back of the computer and when it materialized dragged a remote access app to Jess's desktop. Double clicking it, she enabled it from her cell phone. She tucked the app in a folder and hid it in the Application folder on Jess's hard drive.

"Well, I know how important it would be to Mindy, is all," her mother said loudly, as if in response to something Jess must have said. Mindy stood up and grinned.

It could not have been easier.

*****

Jim Martin's neighborhood was a new subdivision tucked into an older part of Druid Hills that had been razed and rebuilt. Unfortunately, the street itself hadn't been updated and Mia drove around potholes and cracks from thirty years of hard use as she looked for the address. Each of the stucco houses looked enough alike to be virtually indistinguishable from each other, styled in vaguely Mediterranean influence with rounded garage doors and archways.

The page from the file that Mia photographed also included Martin's religious denomination. He was Catholic, which would make things easier for Mia. Everyone who knew anything about Druid Hills knew the Immaculate Heart of Mary Catholic Church off Briarcliff in the neighborhood.

If the guy really was Catholic, that would be his parish. Mia looked up the name of the pastor on the Internet and memorized a couple of the names of the deacons too for good measure. It was a weak ruse but it was all she had. She parked her car in the driveway of a bland, innocuous home that matched Martin's street address, walked to the front door and rang the bell.

A woman in her early sixties answered the door.

"Mrs. Martin?" Mia said. "I'm Mia Kazmaroff, from the parish?"

The frown on the woman's face melted away and she opened the door wider.

"Oh, thank you for coming," she said. "Please come in."

Mia stepped into the foyer. It had a soaring ceiling intended to give the feeling of space but, unfortunately, the walls on all sides were crammed full of amateur artwork and posters, fostering a claustrophobic, closed feeling instead.

"Did Father Matthews send you?" The woman asked, leading Mia into the living room off the foyer. She was thin, her face showing signs of strain and tension. An unpleasant odor was present in the house and Mia had the sudden thought that it might be coming from Mrs. Martin.

"Yes, he did. I'm just here to see how you're getting along and if there's anything we can do for you."

"No, all the casseroles have been very helpful though. I'll never get through them in a month."

"Well, during such a dreadful time as this," Mia said, sitting on the couch and feeling it crackle as if it were stuffed with cellophane, "you need all the help you can. I am so sorry for your loss."

"Thank you."

"I am new to the parish, myself."

"I didn't think I remembered you."

"Can I ask you about Jim? Father is putting together a few words in his honor."

"Oh, that would be wonderful." Mrs. Martin pulled a tattered tissue from her sweater sleeve and dabbed at her eyes. "He was the best son. Never missed a Mother's Day."

"And he lived here with you?"

Mrs. Martin stiffened. "Yes. Just until he got back on his feet."

"Of course. The recession has made it very hard for everyone. Jobs lost, foreclosures…and of course, it's even worse if you have any kind of disability at all."

"I'm sure, although, thank God that was not the case with Jim."

"That's good." *Shit.*

"Can I offer you a Coke, Ms…I'm sorry, how do you pronounce your name?"

"Please call me Mia. Yes, a Coke would be great. If it's not too much trouble."

"Not at all."

"And I hate to ask, but could I use the bathroom?"

Mrs. Martin stopped and looked at Mia with a frown. She glanced down the hall, presumably in the direction of the bathroom.

"I'm afraid, with the pregnancy and all, I have to go all the time," Mia said.

"Oh, goodness, dear. I remember, myself. It's the last door on the left down the hall."

"Thank you."

Mia left her purse on the couch and walked down the hall as Mrs. Martin disappeared into the kitchen. Mia walked first to the bathroom and shut the door without going in, then returned to the first bedroom door off the hallway. The door was closed, and when she touched the knob it radiated sadness and despair up her arm.

This has to be his room.

Inside, it looked like the room of a twelve-year-old boy. It probably was. Little Jimmy Martin's room before he left home as an adult thinking he'd conquer the world and only ever come back to Mom's on Thanksgiving and Christmas.

She needed to hurry. Mia crossed to the bed and felt under the covers, trying to ignore the agonizing shrieks of pain and grief that crept up her arms as she did. *That poor woman.*

She turned to his desk. An ancient laptop lay on top but she didn't bother with it. *How long does it take to grab a Coke and pour it over ice? Hurry, Mia.* Keeping one ear attuned to the possible sounds of footsteps in the hallway, Mia raked open the drawer on the bedside table. Pens, petroleum jelly, a set of Braves baseball cards, a prescription bottle of pills. Her fingers wrapped around the bottle.

"What the hell are you doing?"

Mia whirled around to see Mrs. Martin standing in the doorway, a glass of cola in her hand. Her eyes looked beyond where Mia was standing to the open nightstand drawer.

"I...was just looking for something that Father might use, you know, to talk about."

"Who are you?" Mrs. Martin took a step into the room. "Get out of here. Get out of his room!"

Mia edged past the woman and hurried into the living room. "I am so sorry, Mrs. Martin," she said. "I just wanted to—"

"I am calling Father Matthews right now. He must be a moron to send someone so insensitive to a grieving mother. Get out! Tell him *this* is the reason we don't come any more! Nosy busybodies."

Mia snatched her purse and walked to the front door. As she jogged down the front steps to her car, Mrs. Martin stood on the porch and yelled after her. "And you can tell him to stop sending the goddamn casseroles! I can make better food in my fucking bathtub!"

*****

Mia drove from Jim Martin's house to the parking lot of Ansley Mall, three miles away. Her adrenaline was still pumping overtime from being chased out of the house—a house that vibrated with fury and sadness. It wasn't until she'd driven a good two miles from the neighborhood itself that Mia could fully breathe again.

She looked at the prescription bottle on the car seat next to her, pulled out her iPad again, and carefully typed in *metoprolol* from the label. Within seconds she had her answer. Wanting to bounce out of her seat with barely suppressed excitement, she pulled out her phone and scrolled through her contacts until she found the number for Jack's attorney.

His secretary buzzed her through.

"Murray here," he said, his voice clipped, business-like, and harried.

"Hi, Paul. This is Mia Kazmaroff. I'm calling on behalf of Jack Burton." Murray hesitated so Mia plunged ahead. "I need you to check on something for me. I have reason to believe Jim Martin suffered from…" Mia glanced at the webpage she'd found on her iPad, "…hypertrophic cardiomyopathy."

"Look, Mia," Murray said with a heavy sigh. "I appreciate what you're trying to do. And I know Jack said the guy had a heart attack or something, but the evidence just doesn't support that. I'm sorry."

"No," Mia said patiently, "it wasn't a heart attack. It was Sudden Cardiac Arrest. There's a difference."

"Does Jack know you're calling me?"

"It turns out Jim Martin had a prescription for beta blockers that he filled nearly five months ago, but his bottle is still full."

"And you know this *how*?"

"Listen, all you have to do is subpoena the guy's health records to show he had a heart condition, which he obviously did. A heart condition he needed to take medicine for."

Murray paused. "What was the name of the condition you think he had?"

Mia glanced at her iPad again. "The most common one is hypertrophic cardiomyopathy but it could be one of several. But the point is, if Martin wasn't taking his medicine and he got overly excited, the stress *could* stop his heart."

"Overly excited. You mean like running away from someone?"

"Exactly. If we can prove the guy needed beta blockers in order not to fall down dead when he got stressed out—"

"And then see if the autopsy confirms those meds *weren't* found in his system. I'm with you." His voice had picked up in excitement.

Mia exhaled. "Yes," she said. "Then the ME's report about the spleen is irrelevant because the guy was already dead when it burst. Just like Jack said."

"Do I want to know how you got this information?"

Mia laughed wryly. "Didn't Jack tell you? I'm kinda psychic."

After she hung up with the lawyer, Mia felt a flush of exhilaration. *Anything is possible if you're determined not to give up.* Maybe that philosophy could be extended a little farther? She picked up her iPad and went to the first of six bookmarks for people searches. With a name like Wojinziky, it couldn't be that hard to find an address. Thirty minutes later, Mia closed out the last of her people finding sites. No joy on any of them. She drummed her fingers on the steering wheel and frowned.

An unemployed plumber with a seriously Polish-sounding name. *How is it this hard?* Finally deciding she'd have better luck on a full stomach, she pulled into the drive-through of the nearest Starbucks and ordered a sandwich and a venti iced coffee with four sugars. She had plenty of experience suddenly finding answers to vexing problems the minute she did something else and sure enough, as she was wadding up the paper of her sandwich, it occurred to her: a property record search.

While ol' Jeffy boy might not own his own house—except what self-respecting plumber couldn't afford a five-bedroom Wieland on what plumbers charge?—his parents surely must. She started with Fulton County and by the time she'd searched Forsyth and Cobb, the light was starting to fade. One more county and she'd do the rest from her living room.

DeKalb County. Tanya and Jeffrey Wojinziky.

He's married? Wasn't there a rule against married guys signing up for online dating services? Mia plugged the address into her GPS. It was across town, and with rush hour going on she knew she wouldn't make it there in daylight. Which suited her just fine.

She put the car in gear and pointed it toward the Wojinziky residence.

Between the wedding and Jack's case she hadn't really had a chance to process Victoria's case falling to pieces. One thing she knew as sure as she knew traffic in Atlanta was that with Maxwell's team handling it, steps would be missed and protocol skipped. The case had already fallen off the front page—and the third—and while they'd put a squad on it, Mia was convinced the sad ending of Victoria Baskerville was well on its way to becoming a cold case.

Not if I have anything to say about it. Did the cops even know about Wojinziky? Had they ever questioned him? Had they even gotten that far? She turned onto Ponce de Leon Avenue. The map on her GPS made it look like the Wojinzikys lived in Atkins Park. That was a pretty neighborhood and bordering on upscale for the area. Pretty good for an unemployed plumber.

She turned off Ponce in front of the old Plaza Theatre onto Barnett Street. The azaleas and dogwood down this street clearly hadn't gotten the memo from the rest of Atlanta's foliage and the season. It was an early explosion of pink and cotton-ball white punctuated up and down the avenue as the dogwood and the Bradford pear trees vied with each other for sheer stunning display.

Wojinziky's house was a split-level that had been renovated. The landscaping wasn't professional, but it was mature and lush. There were two cars in the driveway, one of them a pickup truck with a magnetic sign on the door that said *Fast Plumbing*. No wonder she couldn't find him by Googling his name. He was smart enough to know nobody was going to remember *Wojinziky's Plumbing.*

Just as she unbuckled her seatbelt, her phone vibrated. She glanced at the screen before answering.

"Hey, Jack," she said. "How you feeling?"

"A lot better since I talked with my lawyer. Mia, get your ass home so I can kiss you. I can't believe you found out the guy had a heart condition! How did you find out?"

"Oh, you know us private eyes, we have our little ways."

"Tell me you didn't go to his house."

"Hey, don't ask, don't tell, baby."

"Mia, if I wasn't so sick—and so amazed about what you discovered—I'd kick your ass."

"No need to thank me, Jack. Your smiling face is all the thanks I need."

"Seriously, Mia, thank you. I'm just sitting here stunned because I can finally see a way my life won't be a total nightmare going forward and I really need you home."

"I have one quick thing I have to do first. Want me to pick something up on the way back?"

"Where are you?"

"Near Ponce."

"There's a great Thai place near there."

"Call it in then text me the address and I'll pick it up on my way back."

"I love you, Mia."

"I love you, too, Jack. I won't be long."

She grinned and tucked the phone into her purse. Things were working out. It was all just working out. Jack's preliminary hearing would clear him. They'd go back to major snuggle sessions. And he would help her pick up the threads to a case nobody was paying them for and that everyone in Major Crimes would have a major shit fit about if they found out they were still investigating.

Good times.

She left the car and hurried up the cracked sidewalk to the front door. The porch light was on and she could hear noise from the television set. She took a deep breath and knocked. One way or the other, she was going to clap hands on whoever came to the door and get some answers once and for all. The temperature had dropped with the light and she found herself hugging her arms for warmth.

Maybe the murderer would let her warm up inside his foyer for a few minutes while she questioned him?

She knocked again, louder, and began searching for a doorbell when suddenly the door opened and none other than Jeff Wojinziky himself stood on the doorstep. She'd forgotten if she'd read how tall he was but he was big—linebacker big. Much of it was hanging over the front of his belt, but his arms looked like they could lift fully loaded meat hooks. Mia took an involuntary step back.

"Can I help you?" He didn't look particularly menacing, especially dressed in cutoffs and flip-flops, and Mia was about to speak when she heard a woman call from the living room.

"Who is it, baby? I already paid the lawn guy." The woman had the most discordant voice Mia had ever heard. Halfway between a screech and a squawk, the sound made Mia visibly wince.

"It's nobody," Jeff called over his shoulder and then eyed Mia. "Can I help you?" he repeated, much less friendly now.

"You don't remember me, Jeff? We met on *Atlanta Loves*," Mia said brightly. "You said you'd call but you didn't, so here I am. Can you talk?" She was inches from stepping across the threshold to get a hand on one of his beefy Popeye arms, but he lunged out the door and grabbed *her* by the arms.

Before she could catch her balance, he shoved her backward off the porch onto the sidewalk, then jumped down and placed a heavy foot on her neck.

11

"Get the fuck outta here while you can still crawl," Wojinziky said, his voice low and feral. Mia struggled to get out from under his foot but he pressed harder until she froze, her hands clawing impotently against the cold walkway.

For a moment she was sure he was going to crush her windpipe, but he reached down and jerked her to her feet. The movement made her dizzy and her stomach lurched. She felt her sandwich coming up and fought to control the nausea. He held her by the lapels of her jacket until she could stand unassisted. She saw him look over his shoulder at the house.

When he released her abruptly, Mia staggered away, her hand to her throat. The car felt like a very long distance away. She heard the front door slam behind her before she was halfway down the walkway.

A man who can bully women so effortlessly probably doesn't worry about them not obeying him.

Mia reached the car and pulled herself into the front seat, her hands shaking so badly she could barely get the key in the ignition. She drove to the end of the street and turned down a side street in the neighborhood. She pulled the car onto the side of the road and parked. *Don't think, just do.*

Her heart pounding in her throat, she took her Glock out of the glove compartment and fumbled with the door handle. Her legs were still jelly and she leaned against the car for support. It was dark but she would still need to act quickly. Neighbors were always curious and she couldn't afford for anyone to see her.

She slid the gun in the back of her waistband, blowing hard to steady herself and hoping she didn't hyperventilate in the process. She forced herself not to think about what had just happened. She opened the car trunk and found what she was looking for under a tarp and a heavy blanket.

Tucking the electronic tracking devise into the pocket of her jacket, she locked the car and walked across two darkened yards until she was across the street from the Wojinziky home. Her hands were still trembling and she took a moment to calm herself before jogging across the street and squatting behind the second car in the driveway. When she was sure nobody had seen her, she duck-walked to the back of the pickup truck and clamped the magnetized GPS tracker onto its undercarriage. She knew it was against the law to use it on Wojinziky's truck without his permission. She knew Jack would shit three shades of blue.

She flipped on the activation switch.

Keeping low, she ran back to the facing yard and then made her way back to her car. She waited until she was at the Thai restaurant before she opened the browser on her smartphone to activate the tracking service for the device. She touched her throat. Her phone vibrated with an incoming text.

<You nearly here?>

<5 min away.>

<Great.>

Mia dug for a compact in her purse to make sure she didn't look any worse after her meeting with Jeff

Wojinziky. The last thing she wanted to do was spoil what promised to be a joyous evening with Jack with annoying signs of having been attacked by a psycho killer.

She got back in the car, the spicy aromas from the bag of Tom Yam Goong and Pad Thai takeout permeating the interior. Even without touching him, Mia had gotten the answer to her biggest question. It *was* him. She knew it without laying a finger on him. She knew it from his wild, hooded eyes full of fear and shame. She knew it from the way he'd reacted when she told him she was from *Atlanta Loves*—just like Victoria.

Guilt, Jeff. It's the karma that keeps on giving. Mia pointed her car toward Atlantic Station.

Or at least I intend to make sure it does.

*****

Jack didn't know how she did it. Ever since Murray called nearly two hours ago, Jack was caught between frenetic cleaning and cooking to absorb his kinetic joy and sitting and staring into space, dumbstruck that the nightmare seemed to be coming to a close.

He hadn't killed the guy. The ME was wrong. A miracle had just trumped science.

A miracle named Mia.

He stood at the kitchen counter and spooned the chicken sauce he'd just whipped up into six flour tortillas. It was a simple recipe and one he made frequently for his clients. It wasn't filet mignon but it was a favorite of his girl's. He paused in the middle of rolling one of the tortillas to stare—again—out the kitchen window at the Atlanta skyline in the distance.

Can it really be over? Is it possible that Mia bounced out of here this morning to do a bridesmaid's fitting and five hours later I get a call from my lawyer saying there's a major break in the case?

It made sense, of course it did. Why hadn't he thought of it? The guy obviously had some kind of condition. Nobody just drops dead like that. *Was I just so wrapped up in my guilt about my role in his death I couldn't take the step past it to really see my own innocence?*

But Mia did. Even though her eyes told her a different story, she took that extra step.

And found the truth.

Jack topped the casserole with sour cream and shredded cheddar cheese, covered it in foil and slid it in the oven. He poured two glasses of wine just as he heard her key in the front door.

Finally.

He met her in the foyer, pulled her purse off her shoulder and set the bag of Thai takeout on the side table as she slid into his arms. Neither of them spoke for a moment. He thought he could feel her trembling.

"Mia?"

"I'm okay."

He pulled back to look into her face, to search her eyes.

"I can't believe it," he said, his eyes misting. "I can't believe it's over."

"Did Murray say he thought it would be enough?"

"He's pretty certain. Even if it goes to trial now, I'll probably be acquitted. I'm not in the same place I was before you found out about Martin's heart condition."

She looked over his shoulder. "Are you cooking? I thought we were eating Thai."

"I don't know what I was thinking," he said, scooping up the bag of takeout and leading her into the kitchen. "You don't even like Thai."

"Oh, Jack, you're making me chicken enchiladas?"

"I am." He handed her a glass of wine as she sat at the counter. "How did you do it, Mia?"

She let out a long sigh. "I heard somebody talking about dropping dead suddenly and I thought, wow, just like the guy with Jack. As soon as I opened up the possibility of it, I just followed it down the rabbit hole as far as it went."

"And did it go to Jim Martin's house?"

Mia grinned. "I may have felt the need to offer my condolences to the family, during which time I may have felt the need to rifle through Martin's dresser drawers."

Jack leaned across the counter and kissed her mouth. She tasted of wine and peppermint.

"What else happened today?" he asked softly.

She took another sip of her wine and let her coat fall to the floor behind her. Normally, he'd fuss at her or pick it up himself. Not tonight.

"Jack, I cannot let go of what happened to Victoria Baskerville."

"I figured that."

"Maxwell's crew is not going to solve it, I just know they're not. They're not even looking in the right direction."

"What direction is that?"

She looked uncomfortable which gave Jack a prick of concern. *What had she been up to?*

"I think I've found a person of interest. Of serious interest."

Jack touched her chin where he could see a bruise forming. Mia took his hand from her face and squeezed it.

"I'm not giving up on her case," she said. "And I know Maxwell wants me to back off and that none of the files are available to me and nobody's paying me to investigate but I don't care. I need to find the truth."

"You mean *we* do."

"Really, Jack?" Her look was wide-eyed and hopeful and Jack felt a twinge of guilt that he'd taken her to the point of believing he didn't care about what she cared about.

"*Really*, Mia. How about we have a great meal, then go over every inch of Victoria's case file? The one you're not supposed to have? Would that make you happy?"

She jumped up and ran around the counter to slip her arms around Jack's waist. "I'd say that qualifies as downright foreplay."

He laughed and kissed her. "Mia, darlin, you are truly one in a million."

*****

The pair of dolls lay nestled in the tissue paper, their little plastic faces mottled with the dried blood.

"You think it's real blood?" Mia asked Jack, who stared at the box with his mouth hanging open.

"Yes," he said finally.

"Well, I've tried to think of who might have sent it, or why, but I keep coming up empty. It's a message, right?"

"It's a warning, Mia."

"Are you sure it isn't a brag? Like the killer trying to rub it in my face?"

Jack dragged a hand through his hair and stood up. Daisy came to the coffee table and sniffed at the box. "Get away from there, Daisy," he said sharply. "I have no idea what goes through the minds of seriously deranged people. When did you say this came?"

Mia frowned and tried to think. "Four days ago?"

"Before Cook was released?"

"Yes. Although it still could've been from him, I guess."

Jack sat back down and looked at the box. "It's definitely supposed to be the twins," he said and then looked up at her. "Shit. You didn't tell Maxwell, did you?"

"You think the twins are in danger?" Mia felt her heart speed up. Why hadn't she taken the dolls straight to the chief? What was she thinking?

Jack was already on his phone. "Hey, Chief," he said, his eyes on the bloody package. "We got a situation here. Mia was sent a package a few days ago that might be interpreted as a threat against the twins who worked with Victoria Baskerville on her scams."

Mia watched Jack's face and chewed her nails. Were the twins all right? Why hadn't she connected the dots on the dolls? Why had she only seen it in reference to herself?

"Yeah, okay, good to know. Yeah, I'll tell her." He hung up.

"Tell me what?"

"You don't want to know. Anyway, he says they had a detail watching the twins' house that they just removed and he'll put it back in place."

"Good."

Jack sat down next to Mia and put a hand on her knee.

"I'm sorry you felt you needed to do this without me," he said. "I don't want you to ever think that going forward."

"It's okay," she said, covering his hand with hers. Last night had been a reunion beyond her wildest hopes —not just in bed, which was its own special celebration, but in the support and solidarity that she felt from Jack on working on Victoria's case.

She wasn't alone anymore.

"So Maxwell is going to come pick this up in a few," Jack said, "and I've got the rest of the day at your service."

"Are you cooking for someone tonight?"

"I am, but it shouldn't be late."

"Okay, well, the list I told you about? The one of all the guys Victoria contacted but supposedly never met in person? If you can help me run them down, that'd be great."

"And how many did you say were on the list?"

"Maybe five hundred?"

Jack whistled. "Okay, well, let's get started. How are you going about it?"

"Well, when I had access to Victoria's account I was checking all their profiles and then emailing or calling the contact info that Nathan Turner gave me. Except for the six I told you about where there was no contact info. Them I found through people finder sites—except for Wojinziky, who I found through a property search."

"You have learned well, grasshopper," Jack said, picking up the thick sheaf of names. "And now that we don't have access to Victoria's account?"

"Well, we do it blind, I guess," Mia said, shrugging. "We still have the contact info, we just don't know anything about them."

"Plus, I'm almost positive Maxwell is going to see our involvement as obstruction."

"He's so narrow-minded sometimes."

"Okay, so we call these guys and say what, exactly?"

"Again, a lot harder without access to their profiles," Mia said with a sigh. "I was thinking it might make more sense to visit them."

"Mia, that will take months. Maybe years."

"How can I qualify them on the phone?" she asked. "Without the profiles, I need to see them and, preferably, touch them."

"You're going to touch five hundred strange guys? You're going to knock on five hundred doors, say 'excuse me' to the wife or whoever answers and then slap your hands on five hundred strange men?"

"Pretty much," Mia said with a shrug. "I'll know the killer as soon as I touch him."

"So are you ruling Jeff Wojinziky out? You had physical contact with him."

"It didn't count.   I got waves of anger and resentment off him but I was too busy trying not to skid down the sidewalk on my ass to read him for more than that."

"So you need to see him again."

"I do." She debated mentioning the GPS tracker but decided not to muddy the positive attitude just now with illegal procedure.

*****

That afternoon they drove to the residences of three of the men on the list. By the time they were thrown out of the third guy's condo, Mia had perfected her spiel and her approach.

Unfortunately, it came at the cost of a fat lip to Jack on the last visit. Even so, she could barely contain her excitement on the drive back to Atlantic Station. She had touched three potential suspects, and felt absolutely nothing beyond the usual run of the mill angst or apathy. She ignored any tingle of lust or sadness she picked up in the men. She was looking for a man who had stabbed a young woman twenty-four times with a pair of scissors.

That kind of man would scorch Mia's fingers the instant she made contact with him.

"So, a good day?" Jack said around his swollen lip.

"A very good day," Mia said. "Now we just have to repeat it a few hundred more times—unless we get lucky. The one we're looking for doesn't necessarily have to be the last one we interview."

"He kinda does, Mia," Jack says wryly, "by definition."

"We'll put some ice on your mouth when we get home. And I promise to be extra gentle with you tonight when you get back from your cooking gig. You think you'll be too tired?"

He gave her a side-glance and a crooked smile. "I think you can count on me to perk up," he said dryly.

"I know it's going to take a long time, Jack. But no matter how long it takes, I can't tell you how happy I am knowing that, with your help, sooner or later, we'll find the guy."

He put a hand on her knee. "I know, Mia," he said, "me, too." His phone rang and he picked up. "Hey, Will."

Mia snapped her head toward him. She strained to make out what Jack's lawyer was saying.

"Uh huh," Jack said, not looking at Mia. "Really? Okay. I understand. Okay. Sure. Bye."

He disconnected.

"Well?" Mia said. "Are you going to tell me?"

"Keep your eyes on the road, please."

"Jack!"

"Hypertrophic cardiomyopathy," he said. "No beta blockers found in his system and his personal health records indicated he was being treated for hypertrophic cardiomyopathy."

Mia let out a long sigh. The tension in her shoulders softened.

"Thank God," she said.

As soon as they got home, Jack laid out his tools for his evening and Mia walked Daisy around the parking lot. Being patient wasn't really her strong suit, but she knew, in this case, that finding Victoria's killer was all about the long game. Now that Jack was with her again —in every sense of the word—she could do the tedious work necessary to finally uncover the murderer.

When she came back inside, Jack was in the shower. Mia fed the dog and settled down on the couch with the remote control. It was a little past six in the evening. She put the evening news on and muted the volume, then picked up her phone and dialed her mother.

"Hello, darling, you and Jack still coming to dinner tomorrow?" Jessie sounded tired. Her normal sparkle was missing.

"Of course. Feels like ages since I've seen you. Everything okay?"

"Just perfect, Mia."

"Mindy was a no-show for the bridesmaid's fitting," Mia said.

"I know. She and her mother visited me instead."

Mia sat up straight. She heard the shower go off and she could hear Jack humming.

"You're kidding. Why?"

"Oh, it's just…nothing really."

"They both showed up? Doesn't sound like nothing."

"There's a misunderstanding about my ring, it seems."

"Your ring? The ring the chief gave you?"

"Mindy seems to think her grandmother meant for her to have it."

"Isn't she already married?"

"She is but she has a daughter."

"Her daughter's five years old."

"Nonetheless, Mindy wants the ring for her daughter."

"Mom, this is just her trying to cause trouble. She's about as sentimental as a gallstone. What did you do?"

"I nearly gave her the ring right then."

"Mom, don't even tell me!"

"Well, I didn't. In the end, I felt I needed to talk to Bill first. I mean, he did give it to me."

"What did he say when he heard?"

"He was not happy."

"I'll bet."

"He wants me to keep the ring."

"God, is this some mega-caret monster or something?"

"Not at all."

"So it's sentimental on the chief's part and so has great value. And it's a way for Mindy to make her dad miserable so, again, has great value."

"Anyway, it'll all get sorted out. What's happening on your end? I know you were upset when Bill pulled the plug on the Internet Hussy case."

"Yeah, no, I'm good. Keeping busy."

"I'd like to be there at Jack's preliminary hearing tomorrow."

"I think it's going to be a lot less dramatic than originally believed," Mia said as Jack appeared in the doorway of the kitchen. He was dressed but his hair was still wet. "And I'm pretty sure he doesn't want any of us there."

"Is that your mom?" Jack asked.

Mia nodded.

"Tell her hi from me and not to come tomorrow."

"Tell him hi from me, too," Jess said. "And is he sure he doesn't want support? I'd really like to be there for him."

Jack leaned over and gave Mia a kiss on her neck before retreating to the kitchen to finish packing his chef's cart.

"No, he's good, Mom," Mia said as she watched him in the kitchen. "I think tomorrow's going to be just fine."

An hour later, after kissing Jack goodbye, Mia ran a bubble bath for herself and poured a glass of wine. She meant what she said earlier. Even though they hadn't found Victoria's killer—or even any new leads to follow to that end—it had been a nearly perfect day. She and Jack had worked seamlessly together, very nearly reading each other's minds as each prospect opened the door and endured their questions and, eventually, Mia's touching. It was the kind of easy, synchronized dance that she'd always fantasized would be the reality of her partnership with him.

As she slipped into the hot tub, the fragrant bubbles popping all around her, it occurred to her she'd never been happier in her life. She closed her eyes and soaked until the water was tepid and her wineglass was empty. She toweled off and dressed in yoga pants and a baggy sweatshirt. As far as she was concerned, life couldn't get more perfect than a heated-up dish of Jack's macaroni and cheese—made with four kinds of creamy cheeses—and little Daisy curled comfortingly at her hip. Mia knew the dog's close proximity had more to do with the dish of remaining macaroni and cheese than any strong desire to cuddle, but the effect was the same so she didn't care.

She cycled through two hour-long police dramas, ridiculing the implausible made-for-TV police procedures and the not-to-be-believed turnaround times on lab results and glanced at the clock. Nearly midnight. She was tired. There was something about contentment and hope for the future that was especially wearing. She loved falling asleep in Jack's bed and being awakened by him in the middle of the night—his body hard beneath the warm covers, his hands sure and knowing on her body. She tingled deliciously in anticipation and then eyed the dog. Unfortunately, all this coziness had to be rudely destroyed by a quick jog downstairs to let Daisy wet the ground before bedtime.

"Come on, girl," Mia said. "Let's get this over with."

Wriggling into her coat, she snapped Daisy's leash on her and trotted her downstairs. The night was moonless and cold and it had rained during the evening. Mia opened the heavy front door to the building and ushered Daisy out.

"Get busy," she said. The little dog looked at her and didn't move.

Sighing, Mia stepped outside and led the dog to the edge of the sidewalk, where the animal promptly squatted on the grass. The cold cut straight through Mia's jacket and she hunched her shoulders to make a smaller target for the wind.

So focused on the misery of the cold night, Mia didn't see the menacing form step out of the dark shadows by the building until he was on top of her.

12

Daisy bared her fangs and growled as Joshua Cook took a step toward her. Mia gasped and dropped the leash.

"What are you doing here?" she said, hating how afraid her voice sounded.

"Don't worry, sweetheart, I just want a quick word with you alone. The thing with owning animals—and aren't they such a comfort?—is that eventually you have to come out into the scary darkness. All I had to do was wait."

"You can explain to the police why you felt you had to wait outside my condo," Mia said.

"Waiting in a public parking lot isn't against the law."

"What do you want?" Mia lurched forward to snatch up Daisy's leash again and pull her away from Cook. He was wearing only a thin windbreaker, but seemed impervious to the cold.

"I need to ask a very small favor, sugar, and then I'll be on my way."

Mia glanced at the front of her building but there was little chance anyone would be coming home at this hour in the middle of the week. And Jack wasn't due back for at least another hour.

"Just spit it out," Mia said over Daisy's low-throated growls.

"A phone number."

"Drop dead."

"Fine. I'm prepared to pay you since, for the right amount of money you were only too happy to do so earlier."

"That wasn't for you," Mia said hotly. "I'm happy for you to sit in jail for life."

"Charming. But as the old joke goes, we've already established you're a whore, now we're just haggling over price." Without waiting for her to respond, he pulled out a small handgun and aimed it at her.

Mia took a step backward. "Are you insane?" Her skin tingled uncontrollable. She found it hard to breathe. There was no place to run. He was close enough he could shoot her several times before she made it back to the building.

"Not at all," Cook said. "If you don't know the number offhand, you can email it to me. I trust you. And *you* can trust I'll be back if you don't."

"You are threatening me at gunpoint? You must be out of your mind."

Cook laughed and readjusted his aim from Mia to the little dog. "I'm only doing what anybody would do who was out enjoying a little night air and was then attacked by a dog."

Mia pulled Daisy to her. The fear radiated throughout her chest like a living thing. He could do it and he would only end up paying a fine. She pulled the dog into her arms.

"Shoot her now, you degenerate pervert, and you'll shoot me, too."

"Degenerate pervert is redundant—" Cook said and then slowly crumpled to the ground in front of Mia, his gun skidding across the sidewalk.

Jack materialized behind him still wearing his white's chef's jacket and holding a wine bottle in one hand. He looked down at Cook's twitching body on the ground and then up at Mia, her mouth open in surprise, the dog squirming in her arms.

"This is truly starting to become a habit," he said, shaking his head.

*****

After the police left, Jack and Mia finally fell into bed, exhausted but hungry for each other nonetheless. He let her lead the way but there had never been any doubt. She needed him. She needed his arms around her, she needed the very essence of him embedded deeply within her as she entwined her legs around his waist and drew him closer, tighter, further. He took her hard and completely. To Mia it felt like Jack was ridding himself of the past, his worries, the future and all doubts—all in one perfect connection that ended in tender kisses and murmured words of love.

Even if they'd had to go downtown, which blessedly they did not, Mia knew they still had to connect tonight on every level that was possible. When they lay together afterward, depleted and limp, she couldn't tell where her body began and his left off. A part of her swore never to let him out of her bed again so that reality might never squirm between them.

"I'm going for a glass of milk," he whispered into her ear. "Interested?"

"Chocolate?" she said, stirring and then collapsing back into his arms.

"Can do."

"Only if you can get it without leaving the bed."

He laughed and disengaged. "You'll hardly know I'm gone."

He padded across the room naked. Mia saw the hall light flick on and heard the sounds of Daisy's nails as she follow him into the kitchen. She put a hand in the spot he'd left. It was warm but grew cold as she waited. Her hand felt the spot and tingles of pleasure and bliss sparked off her fingers as she swept the area on the bed. She smiled.

Jack came back with a tray of cookies and two glasses of milk.

"Oh, my God," she said, sitting up. "You really are my hero."

He set the tray down on the bedside table and slipped under the covers.

"I gotta tell you, when I saw that dude standing there holding a gun on you in our own parking lot, this is *not* how I imagined the night might end, with you raking my back and howling *faster-faster* to the rafters."

She slapped him playfully on the shoulder. "You're fantasizing again."

"Well, that's what it felt like, anyway."

"I can't believe they didn't take you downtown, Jack. I was so worried they would."

"You and me, both."

"Did the cops tell you what phone number he was after?"

"I think it was one of the twins," Jack said.

"What a psycho. What will happen to him?"

Jack finished off his milk and took Mia's drained glass from her. "Well, he'll be booked and released on bail sometime tonight or tomorrow morning."

"Do you think he'll sue you for hitting him on the head?"

"I think the whole pointing-a-gun-at-you thing will prevent the likelihood of that particular turn of events. I'm not worried."

"I can't believe he came here."

"Addictions make people do strange things," Jack said as he brushed the crumbs of the oatmeal cookies off the duvet cover and snapped off the light. "And I should know. Come 'ere, you." He turned her in his arms and pulled her into his chest. He ran a hand down her body from her hip to her calf and sighed, content that all was well.

"I love you, Jack," she said. "Thank you for coming home early tonight."

He kissed her ear. "I love you too, Mia. You're welcome."

The next morning, Jack dressed for his day in court and firmly held to his edict that Mia not attend. She sat at the kitchen counter still in her PJs, a plate of buttered toast in front of her.

"Promise me you'll text me as soon as whatever happens, happens," she said, her voice low. She watched him move about the kitchen turning off burners, placing coffee mugs in the sink.

"I will."

"And we're supposed to have dinner at my mom's tonight."

"I know, Mia." He kissed her briskly and collected his phone and keys from the counter. "It's going to be fine."

She followed him to the door, where he turned and took her into his arms.

"Why don't you go back to bed?" he said into her hair. "Then I can think of you there during the boring parts of the hearing." He ran a hand down her bottom and squeezed it.

"I have work to do," she said, wrapping her arms around his neck and rising up on tiptoe to kiss him on the mouth. "But you can still imagine me in bed. And if you do, imagine me naked."

"That's a given." He kissed her again, then turned and left.

Mia fought the impulse to go to the window and watch him drive away. She'd done everything she could and now it was up to the judge—the surely very reasonable judge—and fate and whatever likelihood there was that the ME would swallow his pride and reverse his opinion.

She walked back to the kitchen and picked up her toast but her stomach buckled. She had no control over this day. None. She would say one very earnest prayer that Jack would sail through the prelim, and the nightmare would be good and truly over. After that, she'd put it out of her mind as best she could and focus on finding the men on Victoria's list. *There was nothing like a studiously boring, laborious project to semi-engage the mind and distract you from the possibility that your happiness could be atom-bombed by the end of the day.*

After walking the dog, showering and dressing, Mia looked at her list of men and decided she could handle two visits today without any problem. Having Jack along was easier—and safer—but she couldn't afford to waste a single day. She checked the first name on today's list, a David White, and saw that he lived in Atlantic Station.

Perfect. She plugged his address into her GPS and had just pulled out of the parking lot when her phone began to vibrate. She snatched it up, even though she knew it was too soon to hear from Jack, and saw it was her tracking device activation company.

Wojinziky was on the move.

Her heart fluttered in her throat as she opened the map on her phone to watch the little blue dot that was Wojinziky's truck move from his driveway. She stuck her phone on the holder affixed to her dashboard.

Change of plans.

She drove to the intersection of I-85 and Ivan Allen, pulled off and waited impatiently to see which way Wojinziky was going. The little blue dot hesitated at the intersection of Monroe Drive and Ponce, and then turned into Monroe going south. Mia pulled out of her holding pattern and followed him. When he stopped, ten minutes later, she located him in a grocery store parking lot not far from where he lived. She parked several rows away from his truck and watched him walk into the store.

By the time he reappeared, twenty minutes later, she had her SLR focused on the front of the store. He carried four plastic bags, two in each meaty hand. She photographed him walking to his truck and placing the groceries inside before driving away. Then she sat in the parking lot and watched the blue dot on her smartphone as it returned to where it came from.

As she headed back to Atlantic Station, noting she still had time to knock on David White's door before she had to get ready for tonight, it occurred to Mia she didn't know exactly what she was looking for in staking out Jeff Wojinziky.

But she was pretty sure she'd know it when she saw it.

*****

If he'd just looked at his lawyer, Paul Murray, and nowhere else in the courtroom, Jack would've known with complete confidence that he was leaving a free man. Murray was ebullient and sanguine, shaking hands and visiting with the other attorneys in the court as they waited for the judge, winking at the court stenographer and generally giving the impression of a man who knew a sure thing when he saw it. For someone whose neck was actually on the line, it felt a little less certain.

Two hours later, Jack exited the courtroom with Murray pumping his arm and slapping him on the back, his private investigator's license returned and all charges dropped.

Jack even snuck a quick look at the ME and was greeted by a smile. Nobody wants to be the reason a cop goes to prison. This happy ending was courtesy of a lot of people in the system, he thought, but Mia authored it. And that he would never forget, nor the feeling of walking out into the cold and sunny afternoon on a perfect spring day, a free man.

"Tell your girl she can work my cases any time," Murray said as they parted. "She's a bulldog."

That's one way to put it. Jack walked to his car in the downtown parking lot adjacent to the courthouse and texted Mia.

<It's all over. I'm free and on my way home.>
<That's awesome! Meet me at mom's?>
<Will do. Love you, N>
<Love you, 2, J>

He hurried home to collect his tools and ingredients for the run-through of the rehearsal dinner menu he was making at Jess's tonight.

Two hours later, he pulled up beside Mia's Toyota in her mother's driveway. He saw Jess's car but Maxwell wasn't here yet, which was strange. The man was never late. As Jack was unloading the back of his car—pans, knives and coolers—Mia came running out of her mother's house. He barely had time to turn around before she threw her arms around him. He swung her off the ground and kissed her.

"Hey, beautiful," he said. She grabbed his head with both her hands and kissed him hard again.

"I can't believe it's all over," she said, her voice low and full of emotion.

"I know. Pretty damn great feeling."

"What about the civil suit?"

"Let's enjoy our pleasures one at a time, why don't we?"

"They didn't drop it?"

"Not yet. Murray is confidant they will once all the evidence comes out. I'm not worried so for God's sake don't you be."

"If that's your subtle way of telling me not to go back to his house again—"

He kissed her to stop her from speaking.

"As much as I will always be grateful to your bull-in-a-china-shop methods," he said, giving her a squeeze, "you still scare the shit out of me most of the time."

"Good," she said with a laugh. "What can I help you bring in?"

"Whatever you can carry. The chief isn't here yet?"

Mia pulled a heavy casserole pan out of the trunk. "No and Mom's acting strange, too."

"You didn't mention the whole *being-held-at-gunpoint* thing, did you?"

She made a face. "No, I don't think it has to do with me this time."

"Well, that's progress," he said.

*****

Mia worked next to Jack for the rest of the evening preparing the menu. At their place in Atlantic Station he normally shooed her out of the kitchen. Tonight, she got the definite impression he didn't need her help so much as he just wanted her in the same room with him. Which suited her fine.

Her mother, on the other hand, was distracted—her smiles forced. Mia had been so busy lately that she hadn't asked how the engagement ring issue was resolved—if it had been. She noticed Jess was still wearing it.

Maxwell showed up a full hour after he'd been expected. He went straight to Jack to congratulate him on the results of the preliminary hearing and then to the living room to turn on the evening news.

That was different, too.

Jess didn't seem to mind, so perhaps this was their new routine. People can't stay besotted newlyweds forever, Mia reasoned. *But maybe they could at least make it to the stage of being newlyweds?* She set the table while Jess and Maxwell sat in the living room watching TV. She couldn't hear what they said, and most of the time they didn't appear to speak.

Jack had outdone himself on the rehearsal of the rehearsal dinner. Because Maxwell had left the choices up to Jack and Jess, it had a definite Asian flair to it. Otherwise it would probably have been barbecue. Mia moved into the kitchen, where Jack was pulling the Chilean Sea Bass out of the oven.

"Oh, my God, that smells awesome. Are you really going to be able to do this for fifty people?"

He laughed and tossed down a potholder.

"What is it you think I do most nights when I leave to cook for my clients?"

"Dinner parties for fifty?"

"Not every night but often enough."

"How can one person do that?"

"I have a staff for those events."

"I did not know that. They hire servers?"

"And sous chefs, whatever I need. It's great to be rich."

"I'll say." She slipped into his arms and kissed him. "Why can't I stay away from you?"

"I don't know," he said, kissing her back. "Especially since I have the same problem."

"We about to eat any time soon?" Maxwell called from the living room.

"He's in a terrible mood," Mia said, disengaging from Jack.

"I noticed. Your mom mention any reason why?"

"She just said they were working something out."

"Clearly. Here, take that into them, will you?" He pointed to a tray of miniature corn dogs on a lace doily. "It should tide them over a few moments longer."

"This and alcohol," Mia said, picking up the tray.

"I'm on it."

Fifteen minutes later, the four of them were seated at the table, the wine poured and a selection of hors d'oeuvres and seafood on the table.

"It all looks beautiful, Jack," Jess said, surveying the sparkling crystal and china. "And smells even better."

"Some of it is a little spicy," Jack warned, serving up a section of vegetable *shumai* onto Jess's plate.

"Oh, I think we can handle it," Jess said teasingly, her eyes going to Maxwell, who was busy scrutinizing the sea bass on his plate. Mia passed him a plate of poached bay scallops with *limoncello crème*.

"So, Jack," Maxwell said causally, taking the plate from Mia, "I hear our girl's been busy." For a moment no one spoke. Out of the corner of her eye, Mia saw Jess look at Maxwell with interest, her face open but questioning.

Oh, no, you wouldn't. Mia watched as Maxwell nailed her with a look that eliminated any doubt of what he would or wouldn't do.

"Busy how?" Jess prompted.

Maxwell turned to look at Jess. "Seems our latest prime suspect in the Victoria Baskerville case paid her a visit last night—at gunpoint."

Jess gasped and snapped her head to look at Mia.

"Why did you have to put it like that?" Mia asked him.

"I'm kind of wondering the same thing, Chief," Jack said, a frown on his face.

"A murderer pulled a gun on you?" Jess said, her voice tremulous. "Where was Jack?"

"Jack was sneaking up behind him with a full Merlot bottle," Mia said.

"Bite your tongue, girl," Jack said. "It was a Pinot Noir."

"This isn't funny," Jess said, turning to look at Maxwell.

"Hey, don't look at me," he said. "I just sit on the sidelines and pick up the pieces."

"Boy, it would be great if you were that passive," Mia said pointedly.

"Did I or did I not tell you to butt out of this case?" Maxwell said to her.

"What part of *he came to me* is confusing for you, Chief? I was walking the damn dog, minding my own business, which, if you bothered to read the report, you'd know."

"What I know, Mia, is that I told you to stop investigating this case and you blatantly disobeyed me —"

"Hey, that's a little harsh, Chief—" Jack started.

"And it's a little bullshit, too," Mia said hotly.

"Mia, please!" Jess said.

"Did I or did I not tell you to let the police handle it?" Maxwell said.

"You mean like how you handled it by arresting the wrong man?"

"I don't care who we arrest," Maxwell roared. "That's none of your concern!" He turned to Jack. "Keep her in check or I swear to God I'll arrest her if she goes anywhere near anyone connected to this case."

"On what charges?" Mia retorted. "Or are those irrelevant these days?"

Jack leaned over and grabbed Mia's hand. He leveled his gaze at Maxwell. "Both of you calm down right now," he said.

"You said half the time the cops can't give the necessary resources to a case," Mia said, her face flushed with intensity. "You probably don't even give a shit who killed Victoria Baskerville."

"Mia, stop speaking," Jack growled. "Put it back in the box or I'm taking you outside for a walk, and it's cold as shit out there."

Mia glared at Maxwell. Jack and Jess quickly passed dishes to distract them.

"What is this, Jack?" Jess asked, pointing to a plate of mini sandwiches.

"Those are lobster rolls on brioche," he said. "With *crème fraîche*."

"They look wonderful, don't they, Bill?"

Maxwell stared at his plate. He was clearly determined to keep his sour mood alive. The same sour mood he'd walked into the house with. Mia decided not to sink to his level.

"Corn dogs?" she said to Jack. He grinned and gave her a wink for her effort.

"Jalapeño corn dogs with gingered damson plum sauce," he said.

She bit into one and her eyes instantly watered. "Mm-mm, delish."

"What do you think, Bill?" Jess reached over to touch his sleeve. He glanced at her and pulled his hand away to flap out his napkin across his lap.

"I think the whole family's crazy," he said.

Mia felt Jack's foot on hers but he needn't have bothered. She just figured out what the real problem was and it had nothing to do with her. She watched her mother assess the situation.

"Careful dear," Jess said lightly, removing her hand, "it is, after all, the family you're about to join." Later, Mia would remember the next words like they were the lighting of a fuse.

"So let me ask you, Jess," Maxwell said abruptly. "Did you offer to score pot for my daughter?"

Jess's face went white, her eyes round. "What?"

"Mindy showed me the note you sent. I know you're a little on the avant-garde side, but come on, you do remember I'm a cop, don't you?"

Jess stood and dropped her napkin on the table. "I'm not feeling well," she said.

Mia turned to Maxwell. "Are you serious? Have you had a stroke?"

He turned his attention back to Jess. "Did you or did you not send Mindy the note? How else would she have gotten hold of your stationary?"

"I believe I'm finished for this evening," she said. "If you'll excuse me." Jess turned and walked from the table to the hallway, where they heard her bedroom door close.

Maxwell threw down his napkin and Mia turned on him.

"Get in there and prostrate yourself in apology," she said, in a low growl. "I don't care what you saw, you should know her better than that."

He looked at her and then the hallway and faltered, his face flushed.

"*Mindy* showed you this note?" Mia asked patiently.

"Yes." He continued to stare in the direction Jess had gone.

"I'm sure Mom sent her *a* note, Chief. But if you're saying you think she offered to deal drugs—*I don't care what you saw with your own eyes*—you might as well just leave right now."

The guilt and realization formed on his face as her words hit him. Whatever was going on between these two had been building for days. And if that bitch Mindy wanted to drive a wedge between them, she'd just scored a slam dunk.

"Major fuck up, Chief," Jack said, shaking his head.

Maxwell stood and rubbed his hands on his jeans, his eyes on the hallway where Jess had disappeared. "Shit," he said. "I don't know what's wrong with me."

"Go! Go!" Mia urged, standing and picking up her dinner plate. "Come on, Jack. In case there's screaming, I don't want to hear it. And if there's make-up sex I *really* don't want to hear it." She moved into the kitchen. Jack slapped Maxwell on the shoulder, then picked up his plate and followed her.

Maxwell hesitated, as if rehearsing the words he might use. He was still standing there when Mia came back to the dining room for another armload of dishes. His phone rang. He looked at the screen and then answered it.

"What's up, sweetheart?" he said.

Mia stood next to him and openly listened to his side of the conversation. He felt in his jeans pocket for his car keys and began to move toward the door.

"Okay, calm down, Mindy," he said. "Tell your mother I'll be there in a few minutes. If you get there before I do, move her away from the booze." He hung up and turned to Mia. He gave a helpless shrug and one last look in the direction Jess had retreated, and left.

"Where'd the chief go?" Jack said as he walked in from the kitchen.

"You're not going to believe this. He left."

"What? No way."

"He did. Mindy called with some trumped up story and he bolted."

"Not good, Mia."

"Tell me about it." She looked toward her mother's bedroom.

"Give her some time," Jack said, touching her elbow. "Help me in the kitchen and let her sort this out at her own speed."

"What is *wrong* with that guy?" Mia said in exasperation as she picked up plates from the table.

"He's just trying to keep all his loved ones happy."

"Well, surely he knows by now *that's* never going to work."

They worked silently for the next twenty minutes clearing the table, stacking the dishwasher and securing all leftovers in containers in the refrigerator. As Jack was wiping down the counters, Mia shook off her concern over the fight and came up from behind him. She put her arms around his waist.

"I don't want Mindy's mischief to hijack your amazing news," she murmured into his back.

He dropped the sponge and turned to pull her into his arms.

"I'm riding pretty high at the moment," he said, his eyes glittering. "It would take a whole lot more than that to ruin tonight for me."

"I'm glad." She kissed him deeply and felt warmth spread through her chest. "I intend to fully celebrate with you later at our place."

He rubbed his hands down her back and kissed her neck. She pulled back and frowned.

"Something's vibrating down there," she said, "and I don't think it's me." He grinned and pulled his phone out of his jeans pocket.

"That's weird," he said. "It's the chief."

"He's calling the wrong person then," Mia said acerbically.

"Hey," Jack said into the phone. "What's up?"

Mia moved to the refrigerator and pulled out a can of Coke. By the time she turned around to ask Jack what Maxwell wanted, she saw his face had gone serious, his lips pressed in a tense line. A sudden needle of panic invaded her heart.

"Yeah, I'll tell her," Jack said, his eyes on Mia's. He nodded and closed his eyes, the exhaustion of his very full day finally catching up with him. He hung up and stood holding the phone in his hand.

"What is it?" Mia whispered, afraid to know the answer. "What happened?"

"They found a body an hour ago," he said, moving across the kitchen to take her into his arms. "It's one of the twins."

13

Mia held Daisy in her arms on the couch. For reasons she couldn't name, she'd wanted to stay at her mother's. Maybe she just felt protective. It didn't feel right walking out of the same door that Maxwell had. Not when there was so much sadness inside.

"Was it me? Because I didn't hand in the dolls sooner?" She looked at Jack as he handed her a peppermint tea and slipped into a spot next to her on the couch.

"It wasn't you. Maxwell said they had a uniform watching the house."

"Then how?"

"She slipped out. You can't protect someone who doesn't want it."

"That poor girl. Her poor mother. Her poor twin. Why do I feel responsible?"

"I don't know, darlin,' you shouldn't."

"If I'd found the killer before now…"

"We don't know that it's the same guy."

"Oh, it's the same guy. You know it is."

"Maybe."

"Where did they find her?"

"Are you sure you want to hear all this, Mia? It's already been a long-ass night. I think you should drink your tea and go to bed."

"Are you staying?"

"Of course."

She set the hot tea down on the lamp table and put her arms around him.

"Tell me, Jack, please," she said.

He sighed. "She was found in an alley downtown about two hours ago."

"Stabbed?"

He hesitated. "Yes."

"Do you know when they released Cook?"

"Maxwell said he was in custody during the time of the murder."

"Good alibi, I guess."

"About the best."

Which twin was it? Was it Stacy, who was so serious and reserved and wounded? Or Tracy? The one with all the energy and bounce. Who would do this and why? Jeff? Mia had checked her tracker but Jeff hadn't left his house all night. Did that mean it wasn't him? Maybe he borrowed his wife's car? Why hadn't she thought of that?

That poor girl. Her poor, poor mother.

Jess's bedroom door opened. Mia waited for her mother to appear in the hall off the living room. Jess was in her robe and her makeup was washed off. She looked like she'd been sleeping.

"What happened?" she asked.

"One of the twins in the Baskerville case was murdered," Jack said. "The chief had to go."

Might as well make her believe that as opposed to the real reason.

"Oh, that is terrible. Her poor mother." Jess looked like she was going to cry, herself.

"Jack and I are staying tonight," Mia said. She watched her mother's face brighten a little.

"Oh, good, dear," she said, smiling bleakly at Jack and then back at her. "I'm glad."

*****

It rained the day of the funeral.

Tracy Kilpatrick was laid to rest in a simple casket in East Shadowlawn Memorial Gardens off of 87 Scenic Highway in Lawrenceville. Maxwell had warned her there would be a significant police presence at the burial, and there was. Most of it was the little fourteen-man police force of Lawrenceville, but Mia spotted two detectives from the Atlanta Major Crimes division, as well as Maxwell, himself.

She held Jack's arm as they walked across the grass to the burial plot. Her shoes would be ruined with the mud but it didn't matter.

Tracy's whole life was ruined.

Jack reminded her that every single person at Tracy's funeral would be watched and vetted in the hopes her killer couldn't resist attending. The cops were paying their respects, but they were looking for the bastard who did this, too.

"Did you see the chief?" Mia whispered to Jack as they approached the gravesite. "Mom wanted to come but he didn't want her to. I'm really starting to worry about those two."

"He's just being protective," Jack said.

It had been many months since she'd seen Jack in a suit and tie and she forgot how handsome he was when he was dressed up. When he was a detective on the force, he wore a suit every day.

Rhonda Kilpatrick was visible from a great distance. She stood between Derek and Stacy, leaning heavily on Derek, her bulk sagging against him. At one point, Mia feared she would topple into the open grave.

"That's the mother," Mia whispered. "She's devastated. Poor woman."

"Is that Derek?" Jack asked. Mia had had to come clean about her run-in with Derek Kilpatrick. It hadn't been a happy beginning to their day.

As if going to a funeral was the happy beginning to anybody's day.

Mia strained to find somebody she recognized. Aside from the Kilpatricks, she spotted Bill and Debbie Olds, hanging back—they weren't really friends after all—but in respectful attendance. Mia watched Derek lead his mother to one of the folding chairs in front of the gravesite. She found herself hoping it wouldn't collapse under her. As terrible as Mia felt about today, she knew she was one pratfall away from hysterical, and extremely ill-timed, laughter.

Derek left the seat next to his mother free and took a chair behind her.

That's odd. Someone else besides immediate family rating guest of honor status?

Mia and Jack stood back far enough to be observers without being noticed. A middle-aged woman walked past them. Her back was straight, her hair unfashionably long for her age, her face a mask of unshed tears. She walked to the chair next to Rhonda, squatted down and embraced her.

"Who is that?" Jack asked.

"I have no idea." Mia glanced over at the Olds and wondered if it was bad taste to ask them for a who's who at the gathering.

"Holy shit."

Mia snapped her head around to see what prompted the outburst from Jack, and when she saw the guest she nearly repeated it herself, only louder.

"What the hell is he doing here?"

"I don't know but it's not good," Jack said as they both stared at the impassive, cool form of Joshua Cook standing several rows behind where the Kilpatrick family was seated.

"The chief's seen him," Mia said, her voice rising in her excitement. Maxwell's face was a thundercloud of intent as he spoke out of the side of his mouth to the uniformed man next to him. Cook had just settled into his seat when two plainclothes detectives flanked him and pulled him to his feet. Mia and Jack were close enough to hear Cook's protestations, but the detectives dragged him to the parking lot before too many people noticed the disturbance.

"Why do you think he was here?" Mia asked as she watched Cook being hauled off.

"Who knows? Best not to creep into the brains of people like him."

They turned their attention back to the service. A minister stood in front of Rhonda and spoke in a low voice, his words not carrying to where Mia and Jack were. The rain came down harder. Most everyone had umbrellas, but Mia was surprised to see Derek holding a large one over his mother and sister. He hadn't struck her as the conscientious type.

If it weren't for me, we wouldn't be here. Tracy wouldn't be here. If I'd gotten the dolls to the police as soon as they were delivered, the monster who did this might not have gotten to her.

"You okay, Mia?" Jack wrapped an arm around her waist and pulled her to him. "Not getting too wet?"

"I'm fine."

"This wasn't your fault, Mia."

"I know."

But of course it was.

The woman who greeted Rhonda settled into the empty chair next to her. There were about forty people standing or sitting, listening to the minister. Rhonda's weeping was loud and constant. Stacy sat next to her mother, her back straight, her eyes dry, as if stunned. An older woman with harshly dyed auburn hair leaned over Rhonda to speak to her while the minister orchestrated the removal of the flowers on the coffin.

"Looks like things are wrapping up," Jack said as people turned from the gravesite to hurry back toward the parking lot. Maxwell still stood off to one side. "The chief's not going to be happy we're here," he said.

"I don't care," Mia said. "If he'd caught Victoria's killer before now maybe none of us would be here."

Derek turned to glare at Mia and she found herself glad to have Jack next to her. He was taller than Derek by nearly six inches. The woman sitting next to Rhonda leaned back and caught Derek's sleeve. He turned to speak to her and then pointed to Mia.

Surprised, Mia watched the woman fix a stony glare on her. A relative? The woman turned to pat a still-weeping Rhonda on the shoulder, and then got up and began working her way through the crowd toward Mia.

Who the hell was this? Mia stiffened and Jack looked down at her.

"What is it?" Jack asked.

"I'll let you know in a minute," Mia said, barely moving her lips, her eyes never leaving the woman's face as she approached.

The woman stood in front of Mia, her eyes glancing uneasily at Jack as he towered over both of them.

"You a friend of Vickie's? Is that right?" she asked.

"And you are?" Mia asked sweetly.

As the woman leaned in Jack automatically stepped between her and Mia. She backed off but her tone was no less aggressive.

"I'm Vickie's ex-mother-in-law is who I am," she said. Mia was close enough to tell the woman had been drinking. She was missing several bottom teeth and her makeup looked like it had been applied by someone with palsy.

"Alice Smith?" Mia asked.

The woman gaped. "You know who I am?"

"I've heard bits and pieces."

"You stay away from Rhonda Kilpatrick, you hear me? I don't know what paper you work for, but it won't be worth a stay in the hospital, do you hear?"

"Is that a threat, Mrs. Smith?" Jack said smoothly. "I'm a police officer."

Alice looked at Jack with a worried look and then at Mia.

"I didn't mean it like a threat," she said. "I just meant it as information, like. Rhonda Kilpatrick's suffered enough for her big heart, having her young 'uns with that tramp, Vickie. You stay away from her."

Without waiting to see how her words were received, she turned and walked back to the gravesite. Derek stood with his arms crossed, watching Mia.

"Who the hell was that?" Jack asked.

"Somebody who hated Victoria," Mia said, feeling the gravitas of the day like a dead weight around her shoulders. "That's all."

*****

The child snorted and rolled over in her bed. Mindy stood at Bethany's bedroom door and held her breath. She only got a scant ninety minutes a day when the girl would concede to a nap and Mindy wanted every second of it. After another moment, it was clear the baby monitor had given a false alarm. Bethany wasn't awakening early after all. Mindy shut the door and tiptoed back to her office off the dining room.

It had been a long time since she'd had a project this exciting. Every moment she was away from it, she found herself thinking of how she'd handle the next piece. Every moment she was actually working on it, she was happier than she ever remembered being. She cracked her knuckles and leaned back in front of her double set of video screens. Playing with video editing software wasn't really her strong suit, but she was at least as good as the average TNT producer.

She pushed a button to render the piece she'd just finished editing and sat back and smiled as she waited. Who was she kidding? She was brilliant at it but it didn't matter. None of what she did best mattered. Not to anyone who knew her anyway.

After hitting the Play button, Mindy crossed her arms and watched the video on screen. It was jumpy and the resolution was muddy but she knew most people didn't look at things the way she did. Half the time she had to remind her husband to turn the channel to HD to watch their movies. He really didn't see the difference. It was unfathomable to Mindy, but she'd had too much evidence not to believe it wasn't true.

She looked over her shoulder to make sure little Bethany hadn't decided to turn off the baby monitor—

she'd done it before—in order to creep up behind Mindy while she was working. Today was one time Mindy could not allow that to happen.

She turned her attention back to the video. The woman on the screen arched her naked back and mounted the man. Mindy turned up the volume. And smiled.

The day her father threw her a bone by asking if she would create a video for the wedding was the day Mindy felt lightness return to her step. She had no doubt the so-called engagement would implode long before the wedding, but just in case it got that far she had the back-up plan to end them all.

Because when the congregation—not to mention her father—got an eye and earful of *this* little *Citizen Kane*, well, the only union that would be happening then would be the one where her father's shoe leather met the pavement as he left the church at a dead run.

Mindy watched the two-minute video, the grin never leaving her face. It hadn't been difficult to find a sex tape just shadowy enough to pass—the production quality of most amateur videos was shit. But to find someone who could pass for Jess this perfectly? It had taken weeks of searching through countless user-content video sites to find it. Then with just a little shadowing, a bit of selective cropping and a lot of audio magic—using Jess's real voice thanks to Mindy's most recent visit with her—and even Jess will think it's her up there on the screen, her legs wrapped around the cute surfer dude, riding him while crying out, "Oh-oh-oh! Take me, daddy!"

A part of Mindy almost wished things would get as far as the wedding day.

Oh baby, oh baby.

*****

The rest of the week was a rush of client dinners that kept Jack running off his feet—but happy. He noted that Mia was quieter than usual, which was a tad worrisome, but she didn't seem to be actively hatching any plots so Jack decided not to overthink things. He knew she wasn't through with the Victoria case and maybe that wasn't a bad thing. It kept her occupied. They'd gone out two days in a row to meet guys from Victoria's list and Mia had placed her hands on them. All five had proven to be innocent—in Mia's mind—and Jack hadn't gotten punched.

So win-win for everyone.

This afternoon, as Jack was putting together his chef's cart for a formal dinner party for six, Mia sat at the kitchen counter and flipped through a horse magazine. After the third sigh, he stopped packing.

"Mia, why don't you call Ned and go riding?"

"I already did. He has to work."

"Okay, well, go yourself, then. Doesn't he have a horse you can borrow?"

"I might." She flipped the magazine shut. "You know it's going to take us years to get through all the guys that Victoria *didn't* meet with."

"I'm game if you are."

"And you are a sweet man to be game. Thank you. But my point is, there's one guy who she did meet with."

"Jeff Wojinziky?"

"That's right."

"I mentioned him to the chief yesterday and he said they interviewed Wojinziky and that there was nothing, *nothing* to connect him forensically to the murder."

"You talked to the chief?"

"Yes, now don't get pissed, Mia. We were talking about something else entirely, but I know you were concerned that Wojinziky fell through the cracks so I brought him up."

"Where was I when you had this conversation?"

"I don't remember. He also mentioned he'd talked to your mother and they sorted out their little issue from the night before."

"Yeah, my mom told me," Mia said, drumming her nails on the counter. "She knows that evil bitch Mindy is trying to mess things up between her and the chief and, more importantly, the chief knows it."

"You have to feel sorry for her, Mia."

"Well, I don't have to at all. She's a grown woman. She wasn't molested or abandoned or unloved or any of that."

"We don't know what causes people to behave the way they do."

"Probably a good thing." She sighed and picked up her magazine again before dropping it in frustration. "It's just that I *know* it's him, Jack. How many times have I said that to you about something I felt sure about?"

"A million?"

"That is not true. I have very strong reasons for believing it's him."

"Any of it have to do with the tracking device I noticed on your phone?"

She frowned. "I meant to tell you about that."

"You need to remove it before he finds it."

"When I'm finished, I will," she said.

"Are you going to be okay tonight?"

"Of course. Daisy and I are going to watch TV and take a bath. Well, maybe just me in the bath."

He came around the counter and drew her into his arms.

"Don't be discouraged, Mia," he said. "There's a reason why this feels like the long game. You're looking into the stuff nobody else has the patience for. Great rewards come to those who wait."

"Yeah, yeah." She wrapped her arms around his neck and pulled him down for a long kiss.

He groaned and rubbed a hand down her hip. "Be up when I get home?"

"Count on it."

*****

An hour later, after her bath, a reheating of an especially toothsome penne with butternut squash that Jack had made the day before, and a frustrating fifteen minutes in front of the television set, Mia tossed down the remote and looked at Daisy.

"I can't keep doing this," she said out loud. *I can't go through these men one by one when everyone knows the killer isn't in that group. Even Maxwell knows, and Jack surely does, although he deserves an award for going through the motions.*

She got up and went to the dining room table with Victoria's case folder. In the folder were photos of Cook and Jeff that she'd found online, plus Cargill and Turner. Mia spread the photos out, adding a blank one and wrote Derek on it, and tried to see if they formed a picture. She glanced at the wall clock, nine o'clock, then gathered up the photos, Jeff's on top, and exited the condo.

This was crazy but it was at least mildly more productive than sitting and watching cable reruns.

Somebody might have seen whomever it was who delivered the dolls but she'd never know if she didn't ask. It was unfortunate that she didn't have a photo of Derek but the idea that he'd put together naked, bloody dolls of his sisters still wouldn't gel with her. Neither did it seem likely for Cargill. Or Turner. Sighing, she looked at the pictures of Cook and Jeff and finally put Cook's picture behind the others.

It had to be Jeff. The rest of them just didn't make sense the way he did.

She started at the condo on her floor but the furthest point down the hall, intending to work her way back to her own unit. If she didn't have any luck, she'd go floor by floor before giving up.

Better than cable reruns.

The first door she knocked on was answered by a young man—gay from the way he looked at her and held himself. He had a drink in one hand and looked at her with a frown.

"May I help you?" he said.

"I hope so," Mia answered cheerfully. "I live in B-10 down the hall and was wondering if I could show you a picture of someone I think was looking for my apartment?" She pulled out Jeff's picture as she spoke. The man squinted at it and made a face.

"Never seen him," he said in a tone that made it seem like he was glad about that. "But welcome to the building." Then he shut the door.

The next unit was answered by an overweight woman in her mid-forties.

"Hi, there," Mia said, "I live in B-10."

"I've seen your boyfriend in the parking lot," the woman said. "I'm Sheila."

"Hey, Sheila. I was wondering if you've ever seen this man in the building?" Mia showed her the picture of Jeff.

Sheila shook her head. "Sorry, no. What's he done?"

"Just somebody I'm looking for," Mia said. "Have you lived in the building long?" Sheila was dressed in a bathrobe with her head swaddled in a towel. Mia wondered how she felt so comfortable answering the door at nine at night nearly nude.

"Almost four years. I knew your brother."

Mia dropped the stack of photos on the carpeted floor. Why hadn't she thought of that? Dave lived here for nearly two years before he was murdered. Of course people would know him.

"Oh," Mia said. "He left me the condo in his will."

"That's what I heard. I'm sorry about what happened to him. I really liked him."

Mia knew her brother had been a major player so she supposed he might've trolled close to home on a slow night. It was hard to tell from Sheila's tone if she held a grudge or not.

"Yeah, he was a good guy," Mia said softly.

"Hey, but him I saw," Sheila said, pointing to the floor where Mia was picking up the pictures.

A twinge of excitement pinched Mia. She held out the picture of Cook, who she knew for a fact had been at the condo recently.

"This guy?" she asked.

"No, the other dude. With the mustache."

Mia froze and plucked out the photo of Nathan Turner. Her fingers trembled. "Him? You saw him?"

"Yeah, he was wandering the hall on our floor last week. I'd hardly not remember. Very hot."

"Did he...did you notice if he was carrying anything?" Mia said, feeling a burgeoning lightness in her chest. "Like a package of some kind?"

"Now that you mention it," Sheila said, "he was carrying something. I remember because it looked like whatever it was, it was leaking."

14

The next morning, Jack stood next to Mia in the hallway of Nathan Turner's office building in Midtown. He hadn't bothered trying to talk her into giving the information about Turner to Maxwell first. With the way the chief reacted when she even mentioned the Baskerville case, Jack couldn't blame her. She stood next to him, her body tense as if ready to spring.

In fact, that was exactly what she was going to do. Of that Jack was sure.

"He's going to deny it," he murmured to her, his gaze on the door Turner had to exit from.

"I just need to get my hands on him."

"How many times have I heard that?"

Mia tore her eyes from the door for a moment to glance at him. She didn't smile.

"Just teasing, Mia. Lighten up."

"I'm plenty lightened," she said, refocusing on the door just as it swung open.

Turner was a good-looking man. Mia had failed to mention that or maybe she hadn't seen it. Mia's observations were almost always in direct opposition to any normal person's. Turner was wearing an expensive raincoat and carrying a briefcase. When he saw them, he faltered. The shock in his eyes quickly turned into an appraising glance when he saw Jack.

So that part's true, anyway.

"A word, Mr. Turner?" he said as he moved between Turner and Mia. He could feel Mia vibrating in irritation behind him. He just needed to slow her down. Even if this tool *had* delivered a box of bloody dolls to their address, he could still bring charges against them if they weren't careful. Mia pushed past Jack and clamped a hand on Turner's arm.

"Hey!" Turner said.

"We'd like to ask you a few questions," Jack said.

"Call my office if you want to speak with me."

"Why did you bring that box of dolls to my condo?" Mia asked. "Was it a warning?"

Turner's face flushed and his eyes darted between Jack and Mia. "I have no idea what you're talking about."

"The cops have the dolls now," Mia said, hands on her hips. Jack let her move between him and Turner but he stayed ready in case things got out of hand—as they so easily could with Mia.

"They'll get your DNA off them," she said, "so you might as well admit it."

"Get out of my way or I'll call the police." Turner snarled as he turned away.

"They have your DNA, Nathan," Mia called after him as he hurried down the hall. "You make a threat against the twins and then one dies? You don't have to be Columbo to figure that one out!"

Jack put a hand on Mia's shoulder as they watched him leave.

"I assume by the fact that we're not following him out of the building and into the parking lot that you didn't get what you wanted?" he asked in a low voice.

"He didn't kill anyone," Mia said, her shoulders sagging under her jacket.

"Well, good. We can eliminate him and move on. You didn't like him for this anyway."

"But why did he deliver the dolls to me?"

Jack shrugged. "We'll either find out...or we won't. You want me to call the chief or do you want to handle the honors?"

Mia grimaced. "No, I'll call him."

An hour later, they sat across from each other at the Silver Skillet diner downtown and Jack watched her push mustard greens and corn bread around on her plate.

"It's not the end of the world," he said. "Or even the case for that matter."

She nodded but didn't answer. The chief hadn't held back in his fury over her approaching Nathan Turner. Jack knew she wasn't concerned with how mad Maxwell was with her. The case—which had an exciting new piece to it just this morning—was back to cooling off by the second.

"He said they don't have Turner's DNA in the database," she said, "so they can't confirm him for the dolls. And, of course, there's no chance Turner will voluntarily donate a sample."

"Not if he's smart."

Mia jammed a straw in her tumbler of sweet tea and sighed. "I just wish I knew why he did it. How is he connected to this?"

"You mean because you know he didn't kill Victoria?"

Mia looked at him. "He *didn't* kill Victoria," she said. "*Or* Tracy. Or anyone for that matter. I could tell that when I touched him. But he's still involved somehow."

Jack shrugged. "Maybe he's just trying to protect his business? Send the message to the one Nosy Nellie who was keeping the whole unpleasant media mess alive by warning her to back off?"

"Oh, no, you did *not* just refer to me as Nosy Nellie."

But she was smiling. At least there was that. Jack reached across the table and touched her hand.

"I have another chef job tonight. I hate to leave you."

"Don't be silly. I'll be fine."

"No more canvassing the neighbors in our building?"

"You have to admit it was a good idea, Jack."

"Can you promise to hold off any further investigations until I can go too?"

She shrugged and picked up her fork to prod her food without interest. "Sure," she said, but her eyes didn't meet his.

*****

Later that afternoon, Mia threw a bag of carrots and her riding boots into the back of her car. She knew Jack wanted her to give the case a rest—at least for the day—and she wanted to erase the worried look that was on his face so she arranged to go riding with Ned.

Who knows? Maybe being out in the pasture would give her a different perspective on things. It wouldn't be the first time horseback riding had triggered an idea that had been hiding. Plus, it helped to talk to Ned. Not that Jack wasn't good in that way, but Jack took her moods personally—always wanting to fix things—whereas Ned shrugged them off. Mia found, for the most part, that was more helpful when it came to solving problems.

She hopped on I-85, relieved to see the traffic moving quickly, and plugged her smartphone into her car's Bluetooth system. Listening to music was another thing that often prompted a revelation. Music let her mind go into free fall, where ideas tended to bubble to the surface that she didn't even know were in her brain.

The music faded to announce an incoming call and Mia hit *Accept*.

"Hey, Ned," she said. "You at the barn yet?"

"No, that's why I'm calling. I picked up a nail in my tire and I'm gonna have to bail on today."

"Oh, no," Mia said, but she kept the car pointed toward Alpharetta and the barn.

"You're welcome to ride Banshee if you want."

"Thanks," Mia said. "I really need to ride today."

"He can use the exercise. I haven't been out in nearly a week."

"So he's hot, is that what you're telling me?"

"Well, he might be a little full of himself, let me just say that."

Mia laughed, and after a few more moments of conversation they disconnected. She'd miss Ned's company but she did need the ride today, for mental therapy if nothing else. It was a beautiful spring day, cool but clear, and the dogwoods promised to be approaching full bloom in the woods surrounding the barn. If one afternoon on horseback in an Atlanta spring couldn't fix what was wrong with her, nothing could.

Nothing was going to fix what's wrong with Tracy Kilpatrick.

The thought sidled its way into her brain, erupting from the place she'd pushed it for all the days and hours since the funeral.

Who could have killed her? Why?

As she fought to push the thought back down, her phone dinged and she saw that her GPS tracking service was sending her an alert.

Wojinziky.

Mia put her turn signal on for the next exit. She'd traced his path to and from the same grocery store four different times last week—without ever needing to get in her car and follow him. But this time was different. This time he was moving in the opposite direction of the grocery store. She made a quick calculation as she saw him move out of his neighborhood and merge onto Georgia 400. She exited I-85 onto Jimmy Carter Boulevard.

Wherever he was going, she had a feeling she needed to be there for this one. Her fingers tingled as she gripped the steering wheel. What was it that made her know—know in her *bones*—that this time was different? Was this her gift talking? Was this just an extra bonus? A kind of extrasensory perception boost that she'd never noticed before?

The dot on the GPS tracking screen moved relentlessly down Georgia 400 and then exited onto Abernathy Road heading toward Sandy Springs.

Where the hell is he going? Did he finally have a plumbing job? Who the hell does he know in Sandy Springs?

Mia jumped back on I-85 going south, offered up a prayer of thanks that it was moving quickly in this direction, too, and then exited onto I-285 going west. She knew the Sandy Springs area fairly well—it was a major conduit to Atlanta's main shopping districts. Unfortunately, once she got off the main thoroughfare she'd be severely limited as to which roads to take. And the last thing she needed was for Wojinziky to recognize her car.

Suddenly, the dot on the screen stopped past Spalding Drive. There was a string of apartment buildings and condos on that road and Mia felt her heartbeat accelerate at the thought he was meeting someone. She exited 285 onto Roswell Road. It would take her twenty minutes at least, now that she was off the perimeter loop, to make her way up one of the most congested streets in Atlanta. She watched her smartphone screen. The dot didn't move.

Eighteen minutes later, Mia pulled into the apartment complex off Roswell Road and Spalding. Wojinziky's car was parked in the lot closest to the apartment building. Mia took her time finding a spot near enough to his car where she'd be able to see Wojinziky when he returned—but not too close. It was on the second circuit of the parking lot that she got close enough to the car to realize—he was still inside it.

Shit! Had he seen her? She hurriedly parked six parking spaces away and sat, her heart pounding. Why was he still in the car? *He's been here nearly thirty minutes. Is he waiting for someone?* A few minutes later, Mia slipped out of the car to edge closer to where he was. He sat in the driver's seat staring intently at the opening of the apartment building.

He's stalking someone.

Mia crept back to her car and tried to think. Is he staking out his next victim? Is this connected to Victoria or Tracy? Is this someone new? She glanced at her watch. It was only a little after four but already the light was starting to dim. Was he waiting until dark to make his move? The only way to know for sure was to wait with him. If he went inside, she'd call the chief and risk his wrath—until he inevitably threw himself at her feet with apologies when it turned out she'd caught the killer and saved some poor woman's life.

But if he goes inside, the cops won't get here in time.

Mia reached into her glove box where she kept her Glock, until she realized she'd made a deal with Jack not to carry it until she went to the range more. Damn! Should she call the police now? *Before* a crime was committed? That didn't make sense either. No, when Wojinziky finally decides to make his move, Mia would just have to be right behind him. That was the only answer. Even without a gun she could at least scare him off and save whomever he was targeting as his next "Victoria."

Satisfied with this plan, Mia turned on the heat in her car and settled down to wait. An hour later, Wojinziky still hadn't moved. The light had leached completely from the sky, leaving a dark gray cast. It was difficult to see much more than shadows as cars moved about the parking lot. It wasn't one of the poorer apartment buildings on Spalding—but not the nicest by a long shot. Whoever lived here likely had a job of some kind. Most of the cars in the lot were fairly new, if economy-sized. The fact the complex wasn't gated but was close to Roswell Road also told Mia it wasn't in any way upscale.

Mia knew Jack had left for his cooking gig. He'd texted her a quarter of an hour earlier but she hadn't responded. He wouldn't expect her to, thinking she was at the barn. Because she had nothing but time on her hands, she scheduled a text to him to be delivered in the next hour saying she was heading back to the condo. That way, if she forgot to do it—depending on what went down tonight—he wouldn't worry that she'd read his text but hadn't responded.

Suddenly, she saw Wojinziky open his car door. It had been so long since he'd moved that at first, Mia didn't recognize what she was seeing. Sure enough, he was standing outside his car. Mia squinted in the gloom to see what he was looking at. A woman was coming out of the building, a gym bag in her arms. Mia's heartbeat sped up. *This was it!*

Wojinziky closed his car door and moved toward the woman. Mia followed, keeping several yards behind. She knelt by a parked car and watched the woman when she spied Wojinziky.

"Jeff." She sounded breathless and surprised. But not afraid.

"Hey, Beth."

So they knew each other. That fits. He and Victoria knew each other, too.

"Do you have a minute?" he asked.

Mia watched the woman shoulder her gym bag and look around the parking lot, as if trying to find the right words. She was pretty. Probably late twenties, slim, dark hair. She looked a lot like Victoria Baskerville. And weirdly, a little like Mindy Payne, too.

"I don't think that's a good idea, Jeff."

"I just want to talk."

Mia was surprised to hear his voice sound wheedling and sincere. Not at all the same crazed monster who threw her off a porch and put a foot to her throat.

Except he was.

"Jeff, go home."

Yeah, Jeff. Go home to your wife. Even if she does have a voice that would make rabid dogs cringe.

"I miss you, Beth."

"I know. But I can't see you, Jeff. Please don't come again."

For a moment, Mia thought he would attack her. He stood, looming over her, his fists clenching and unclenching at his side as if trying to decide what to do. And then, like someone had let the air out of him, his shoulders dropped and his head sagged to his chest. He turned and trudged back to his car. Mia knelt in the shadows and watched him pull out of the parking lot and leave. She watched Beth on the sidewalk, her shoulders shaking with her tears.

Mia stood and walked quickly to her. "Are you okay?" she called out.

Beth rubbed at her face and took a step backward toward her apartment.

"I'm sorry," Mia said. "I didn't mean to startle you. It's just that I'm a…friend of Jeff's."

"If he put you up to trying to make me change my mind," Beth said, emotion still thick in her voice, but her eyes wary, "you're wasting your time and so is he."

"It's just that I couldn't help notice how upset you are."

"What else is new?" Beth looked at Jeff's retreating taillights and shook her head. "Screw the gym," she said. "I need a drink. Do you want to come in?"

"That would be great."

And so the Good Samaritan gains a toehold in the victim's trust.

Beth's apartment was obviously that of a single woman's. The living room had macramé plant holders, several amateur paintings of cats and a couch in purple velvet. Mia sat on the couch while Beth poured two glasses of wine.

"How do you know Jeff?" Beth asked as she handed Mia her wine.

"Well, it's really my husband who knows him," Mia said, and was rewarded by a nod from Beth as if that made more sense. "Can you tell me what happened to you two?"

"It just couldn't work," Beth said. "I mean it did for awhile. We were even talking about getting married. Did you know that?"

Mia shook her head and tried to keep an encouraging look on her face. *Maybe Beth doesn't know about the wife?*

"You both seem so unhappy," Mia pushed.

"I know. It sucks." Beth took a swig of her wine and the tears were back, streaming down her face. "I really believed we were meant to be."

"But then why not?"

"I shouldn't say," Beth said. "I know Jeff would feel…betrayed if I did. Since I'm the one who broke up with him, I owe him that much."

"I probably already know," Mia said.

"You probably do," Beth said, dabbing at her tears with a tissue. "I'd be very surprised if you didn't."

So is she talking about Jeff being married? Because that doesn't seem to be a very big secret. Or is she talking about the fact that she knows Jeff murdered someone? Maybe even two someones?

Mia pulled a dry cleaner's ticket from her jacket pocket, wrote her cell phone number on it with her name and handed it to Beth. "If you ever want to talk," she said. "I hope you'll call me."

Beth took the paper and then went to a desk in the living room. She jotted down a few words on a notecard and handed it to Mia.

"I don't have a zillion friends," she said. "I'd like that."

"Me, too."

As Mia maneuvered out of the parking lot a few minutes later, her mind was invaded by an unsettled feeling. She and Beth had hugged before they parted, and Mia was able to pick up that Beth was sad. She was definitely on the level about being brokenhearted over losing the love of her life—one adulterous, murdering bastard by the name of Jeff Wojinziky.

What did it mean that Beth wouldn't say *why* she'd broken up with him? What terrible secret was she keeping in order to protect him? And why couldn't she see him for who he really was?

As Mia left the lights and traffic of Roswell Road for a side street, her mind began vibrating with feelings of dread and anticipation. It occurred to her that the sensation had been swirling just beneath the surface ever since she'd gotten into the car, but she'd been so focused on trying to dissect her conversation with Beth, she hadn't noticed. Now the feeling came roaring to the forefront. There was a scent, an alien smell.

Of malignance.

Someone was in the car with her.

15

Something in the back seat moved against her seat at the same time she reached for her glove box. She needn't have bothered. There was of course no gun in the glove box. A man loomed up out of the back seat, his face and shoulders filling her rear view mirror— as did the knife; the very large knife he held to her throat.

"It couldn't have worked any better," Derek said, his breath hot and foul. "You coming to me, just like I'd dreamed it."

He pinched the knife into her flesh and she gasped at the pain. A line of blood trickled down her neck.

"Take 85 to the connector," he said. "Don't try anything. Your boyfriend's texted you twice. What I wouldn't give to send him a photo of your lips wrapped around my dick, but…" He held up her cell phone with his free hand. "You can't have everything."

He tossed the phone out the window.

"Why are you doing this?"

"Did I say you could talk?" He nicked her neck again and again she gasped. She wanted to touch the wound, push him away, keep her burgeoning fear from filling up the car until there was no more air left to breathe. She forced herself not to move.

"You think because I'm from Lawrenceville I don't know Atlanta?" he said. His eyes darted wildly about the car, at Mia, outside at the interstate, the drab grey buildings of wholesalers and factories flying by. "You take an exit anywhere but onto the connector and I'll know."

Mia nodded.

"Have any idea how sick I am of you people from Atlanta? Especially the reporters—most of 'em ain't even from the fucking South—thinking I'm some kind of hillbilly because I come from Lawrenceville?"

Mia licked her lips. He was taking her out of town. Her throat stung with the shallow cuts, reminding her to bide her time and wait before she acted.

"You're the reason Tracy's dead," he continued, his voice rising. "Not me. Wasn't my fault. What with her whoring all over Atlanta like she's all that. Wanting to be just like Vickie. Well, now she's just like Vickie—dead! Just like Vickie!"

Mia felt the blast of his breath on her neck. His high-pitched voice was reverberating throughout the car and slamming into her right ear.

"Not my fault she ended up like Vickie. I just gave her what she been wanting. I didn't get to Vickie, but by God I got to her."

Oh my God. A needle of ice traced down Mia's spine.

He's confessing that he killed his sister.

*****

The text read <Heading back to the condo now. See u soon.>

Jack glanced at his watch. *She's been gone for over three hours, so that's about right.*

202

He was just packing up from his Buckhead client's house. It was a spring buffet for members of her neighborhood garden party—although they'd all eaten indoors. It never ceased to amaze Jack that there were people in the world—now *his* world—who were so rich they dropped two grand on a luncheon for twelve to celebrate the *possibility* of what their hired gardeners might or might not do in the coming growing season.

It would take Jack another thirty minutes to finish cleaning up and loading the car. He and Mia didn't have specific plans for the night beyond the usual— go find another couple of guys who'd contacted Victoria Baskerville but hadn't taken her up on any offers, have Mia touch them, dodge any punches that might be on tap, then go home and heat up the spicy sausage riggies he'd made the day before. He called Mia's phone but it went straight to voice mail. He texted her a quick message. Her phone probably died and she'd forgotten to use her car charger. When she got back to the condo she'd see his message that he was heading to the gym and would see her around eight.

A feeling crept up the back of his neck but he shook it off. History told him that not being able to reach Mia could be a bad thing. To be safe, he could give Ned a call. There was no way *he'd* let the battery die on his phone, but if Jack called Ned then he'd have effectively announced to two people what an overprotective nut job he was. And Mia for sure didn't need any more evidence of how rattled he got when he couldn't reach her. Yeah, the gym was definitely a good idea. Work out some of these issues.

*****

They stopped at the third rest stop south of the city, toward Macon. Derek hadn't told her that was their destination but they'd passed the I-85 exit heading to Alabama so unless he was taking her to Florida for some reason, it was Macon. Mia sat in the backseat of her car, her hands tied behind her back.

The minute he touched her, she knew it was true. The confusion and hatred jumped off him like sparks igniting a fire when he touched her skin. *He had killed.* The sensation raged up and down Mia's whole body, leaving her trembling and weak. He tied a rag around her mouth that Mia once used to wipe up a gas spill.

He secured ripcords he found in the trunk to her hair and the backdoor handle. It kept her half-inclined, her head invisible to anyone parking next to them. Not that there were very many people at seven in the evening in the middle of the week heading to Macon. And rest stops were usually for people on trips. It was ninety minutes from Atlanta to Macon. If you couldn't make it that far without stopping for a Mountain Dew or a pit stop, you were probably in your eighties. And so, not a big help to someone tied up and gagged in the back of her own car.

Derek had made her pull in so he could use the facilities. He dragged her over the back of the front seat, the knife clamped to her throat, slashing zigzags in her flesh in the process. While the chief had given her some basic instruction in self-defense, the knife to the throat was a lesson they had yet to come to.

Mia watched Derek walk to the bathrooms. They hadn't parked in front of the darkened welcome center—but not far from it either. Unless they had dogs to walk most people parked close to the bathrooms. Mia counted six cars in the parking lot when they drove up. She tried to keep calm, to keep her thoughts from ricocheting around her head in distracted, unproductive quivers of fear.

Is this just rape or does he plan to kill me too? He killed his own sister! There is no limit to what he might do next.

As the thoughts swamped her brain, Mia felt her breathing coming faster and faster. Everything about the rest stop looked so normal—not a bit as if it was one of the last places on Earth she would ever see. An image of Jess came to mind and tears filled Mia's eyes.

Stop it! That's not helping. You'll get back to her. Until an idea comes to me or an opportunity presents itself, I need to wait, to watch, and be ready for it.

That thought hadn't completely formed before a car drove up next to where they were parked. She saw both doors open on her side—so a driver and passengers, at least three. She shot her legs against the window and jackhammered it as hard as she could. She heard one of the passengers—*a child?*—scream, startled.

Mia kicked harder. She felt herself getting stronger, her hopes rising with every thud of her heels against the window. Beneath the sounds of the blood pounding in her head and her feet hammering the door, she heard a man's voice, low and reassuring and her fear caught in her throat.

Derek was talking to them. A woman's voice, and then another man's. They were buying whatever Derek was telling them. What if this was her only chance? Mia kicked harder until the door flew open and her feet kicked air. He grabbed her feet and yanked her hard across the seat, her tied hair stopping the movement and wrenching her head back.

He slapped her hard but her long hair covered much of her face and softened the blow, which seemed to infuriate him. He slammed the door and climbed into the driver's seat.

"You want to make the rest of the trip in the trunk, I'm happy to oblige," he snarled, starting the car up and slamming it into reverse. "Just keep it up. There's only one way this is going down. Vickie used me and she used my girls. Yeah, *that's* what I'm talking about, bitch. You *know* what I'm talking about!"

All Mia knew was that they were leaving the only public place they were likely to hit before he drove them to God knows where. If not now, when? She arched her back and thrashed and kicked as hard as she could anywhere she could reach—the back of his seat, the window, the ceiling.

"You crazy bitch! What are you doing? You don't think I'm serious? You want to end up dead? I'll kill you, you bitch! Just like Vickie. Just like fucking Vickie!"

Mia felt the car swerve. She knew they weren't on I-75 yet. Outside she could see only dark trees—the streetlights clustered around the bathrooms at the welcome center were only a glow now.

"You think I'm playing games? Is that what you think?"

The car slammed to a stop and Mia tumbled off the seat onto the floor. She didn't know what was coming next but she knew she needed her strength for it. She waited, her heart pounding, as he bolted from of the car and jerked open her back passenger door. She felt him grab the cords that tied her hair and begin to rip the hair from them. The screaming agony in her scalp vied with the terrible cramping in her shoulders from where she lay on her hands behind her.

The minute she could lift her head, she jumped at him, using her head as a battering ram. She felt it connect with his jaw, but softly, impotently.

Her attempt seemed to light a fuse of fury in him that was palpable in the air of the car. She twisted away from him, but with her hands behind her she only had her feet and her head as weapons. He grabbed her by the shoulders. She ducked her head into her shoulder but could still hear him screaming and cursing, felt the spittle from his lips splash across her face. A blow connected to her mouth, blessedly shooting her into oblivion.

When she swam slowly back to consciousness, she realized it was the agony in her shoulders that had roused her. She couldn't tell how long she'd been out. She groaned and shifted to her side to relieve the pain of lying on her hands in the trunk. Opening her eyes did no good—open or closed, everything was black. The car was moving, the car radio was on but it was low. Something country.

Her chin was sticky and wet. She moved her tongue along her teeth but none seemed to be loose. Her jaw hurt. Her throat. Everything hurt. A wave of desperation and fear began to build in her chest and she took a steadying breath in a shaky attempt to assuage it.

Stay clear. Focus on what you need to do next.

*****

Jack toweled off after his shower. It had been far too long since he'd hit the gym. He'd really worked it tonight until his muscles screamed and his tendons begged for mercy—then scalded it all with a muscle-deep massage in the hot shower.

He felt like a new man. Was that because of the workout and the shower? Truthfully, hadn't he felt that way ever since he walked out of the preliminary hearing a free man? Jack grinned. Or wasn't it really ever since the moment he'd held Mia in his arms and claimed her as his own?

When your life changes so dramatically for the better—beyond any sense of reality or whatever's happened in the past—isn't every day like Day One of a wonderful new world order? He shook his head and opened his locker. *Ready for my Oprah appearance any time now—"How love made me a new man."*

He pulled on a new T-shirt and glanced at his cell phone. And frowned. At first he thought the text must be from Mia. He didn't have that many people he received texts from, unless you counted the girl who cut his hair to remind him of his next appointment. And this was an alert. He didn't remember signing up for any alerts, but Mia with her usual disregard for boundaries might very well have downloaded one to his phone.

He pulled on his boxers, then clicked on the link. Instantly a GPS map opened up showing a dot moving steadily south toward Macon on I-75.

Is this that Wojinziky guy Mia's tracking? Why am I getting the alert? A clammy feeling came over him. His stomach began the initial fluttering of churning. Before reaching for his jeans, he put a call in to Maxwell, who answered on the third ring.

"I need a favor," Jack said when Maxwell answered. His anxiety crept up his arms like a living thing as he clamped the phone between his shoulder and jaw and pulled his pants on. "And you're welcome to never let me forget it if I'm wrong. But I think Mia's in trouble."

*****

With her hands tied behind her, it had taken Mia longer to activate the secondary tracker she kept in the trunk than she'd expected. Now all she could do was pray that Jack noticed the alert—and understood what it meant. Forcing her physical discomforts to the back of her mind, she allowed the rumble and movement of the car to soothe and calm her.

She would need all her strength, all her wits for whatever awaited her at the end of the car trip. Her mind flittered back and forth. Derek said he would kill her just like he did Victoria. *Isn't that what he said? Or words to that effect? So was he the murderer? Why did he kill Tracy? For what possible reason? Why was he doing this? Does he think I'm connected to Victoria in some way? Has he confused us?*

The car slowed and Mia felt it shift direction slightly, exiting the interstate. It stopped for a moment and she held her breath. Derek had turned off the radio. He was getting ready for something. The car made a hard right turn and then accelerated. Mia knew he was taking her further away from I-75. They hadn't driven far enough to make it to the suburbs of Macon, so they were in deep country now. Even the road felt rougher.

Was anyone seeing the alerts? Mia's eyes went to the tracker. She watched its light blink relentlessly, reassuringly. She scooted over to it and wedged it back inside its bag so Derek wouldn't see it when he opened the trunk. The car began to slow and then turned sharply, throwing Mia against the sidewall. There was barely any room to move around or reposition herself —especially with her hands tied. Even if she'd had a gun stashed back here, which she didn't, her hands were tied too tightly to have it do any good. She'd barely been able to manage to flip the activation switch on the tracker.

The car was stopping. She felt it leave the badly paved road for an even bumpier one and then stop entirely. All her efforts to remain calm were swept away in the physical sensation of sitting in the stilled car. Her gag, sopping with saliva, had fallen from her mouth and now hung from her neck. She braced herself with her feet wedged against the side of the trunk. He'd expect her to kick him when he opened the trunk. He'd be ready for her. Or would he? She brought her knees up to her chest and waited. She heard the sounds of his shoes crunching on the dirt and gravel road as he walked to the back of the car. He stood there, waiting. Mia held her breath, her legs beginning to shake with the effort to hold them poised in position.

The trunk unlatched and began to open, the night air pouring into the fetid enclosure. Moonlight gushed light into the trunk, blinding Mia as she lashed out with her feet—hitting nothing.

"Figured you have something like that planned for me, little sis," Derek said, sniggering as he grabbed one of Mia's feet and began pulling her out of the trunk. Her face smashed against the spare tire and she fought to get her other leg straight before he snapped it in two. He grabbed her by the front of her jacket and yanked, banging her head against the trunk lid. Mia cried out, her head spinning with gold and black flecks of pulsating stars.

"Almost done now, girl," he said. "If you make me carry you, I'll cut you first."

Mia's legs threatened to give out beneath her but she struggled to her feet. He gripped her arm and she stumbled alongside him. They were in a dark, uninhabited stretch of countryside. The car was on a dirt road. She could see lights in the distance. Not too far.

Stall him, stall him.

He dragged her relentlessly toward an abandoned trailer set off the road in the weeds. No lights on. No car parked near it. A dog barked in the distance. Mia imagined the farmhouse, its inhabitants sleeping peacefully...so close. Had Daisy been fed yet tonight?

Derek pushed her toward the trailer stairs. She fell against the handrail, feeling his impatience in his grip. *How can I stall him? Should I collapse? Pretend to faint? He'll cut me. Is that better than what's waiting for me inside?*

"Move it, bitch," he snarled, pushing her. He glanced over his shoulder. *He's afraid the car will be seen. So this isn't that remote. How long until Jack found her? Dear God, was he even looking for her?* She crumpled to the ground, her hands behind her, her head bowed. He reacted by grabbing her hair and pulling her head back.

"You think I'm bluffing?"

She knew he wasn't. She felt it in the hand that touched her hair, the fury and hatred that radiated from his fingers to swamp her entire body. It was the touch of a killer. A killer bent on killing again. Her body began to shake and she squeezed her eyes shut.

"Sick," she whispered. She couldn't take much more contact with this kind of evil. It was undiluted, scorching her skin, careening through her head like a crazed pinball.

"You throw up on me and I'll make you eat it," he said, releasing her and stepping back. The relief of his removing his hand was immediate. Her head cleared and she opened her eyes. He was watching the road, looking in both directions.

Was he expecting someone else? Was this a rendezvous? The thought gave Mia a small schism of hope. Not too many people can match this level of depravity. Surely, if someone else comes...

Derek turned and ran up the trailer stairs and wrenched open the door. He stood there for a moment as if sniffing the air inside, then jumped back onto the ground and grabbed Mia again by her hair. In spite of the explosion of pain that erupted in her head, she made her weight go limp. It was her only hope. He kicked her in the stomach. The pain reverberated in her gut. She vomited but only bile dribbled out of her mouth. In the gloom, she saw him draw his knife out of his pocket.

"You better start walking," he snarled.

She forced herself to her feet. He hadn't noticed she was no longer gagged. Was there anybody around to hear her scream?

The trailer was now only five feet away.

She couldn't let him get her in there.

While he wasn't big, he still outweighed Mia by sixty pounds. Before she could make up her mind to fall down again, he wrapped a wedge of her hair around his fist and pushed her ahead of him.

Maybe there was a weapon inside. Jack, where are you?

She stumbled up the stairs, held upright by his ruthless grip on her hair, the pinch of the knife unrelenting and insistent in the small of her back. On the first step across the threshold, Mia tripped. She managed to stay upright but leaned against the doorjamb for balance. Derek cursed and released her to push past her.

The moonlight streamed through a large picture window illuminating the interior of the trailer. A table was knocked over, the chairs on their sides and scattered about the room. Against one wall was a sofa. Derek shoved the table out of the way and grabbed her arm, pinching viciously into her flesh. He tugged her toward the couch.

The time for stalling is done. You missed it. The window is closed.

Mia stared at the stained and battered couch and felt her lunch begin to inch its way up her throat.

"Been thinking about this for about three weeks now," Derek said from behind her. "Take your jeans off. And your underwear."

Don't speak. Let him figure it out. Don't make it easy for him. She turned to him, her hands still fastened behind her back.

He laughed. "Oh, yeah, what am I thinking?"

Derek pushed her down on the couch and stood over her, peeling his own jeans off first. Mia could see he was hard—probably had been the whole drive here —and he wasn't going to wait any longer.

She forced herself to appear as docile as she could, the fear coursing through her in surges. Her arms ached from where she lay with her full weight on them and she tried not to let the pain distract her.

Timing...it's all in the timing.

"You think you're so smart. You and Vickie," Derek rasped, his face flushed with lust and exertion. "Two of a kind. Bitches, both of you."

Let him focus on the end goal. Let him see it, taste it.

As if to punctuate her unspoken words, the buttons on her blouse—strained by her hands being held behind her back—popped. His eyes went to her chest and he grabbed the blouse with both hands and ripped the fabric away, exposing her bra. He pulled her bra down off her shoulders and her breasts sprang free. The air was cold against her skin but she willed the sensation away. She needed to be ready and the timing had to be right.

He licked his lips, his eyes on her bare breasts now not her eyes, and she saw the moment he was ready, when the world dropped away for him and there was only her semi-naked body before him like a juicy T-bone on a plate. He planted both hands by her head to steady himself and hovered over her.

Now! She brought her knee up hard into his groin and caught him solidly. Not waiting for his reaction, Mia squirmed out from under his collapsing form and fought to get to her knees on the floor. His moans were followed quickly by curses.

That meant he was recovering.

She jerked to her feet and stumbled to the door of the trailer, fearing the feel of his hands on her naked back any moment.

"You bitch, I'll kill you slow for this! I'll cut your tits off and screw you and then kill you! I'll see you dead!"

Don't listen, just move.

The path was clear to the door but the door was shut. Mia fell against it and it sprung open, tossing her down the three-step drop to the weeds and gravel below. He was right behind her now. As she scrambled to her feet, she heard him grunt as he jumped down behind her. Her head jerked back as her grabbed her hair.

In the back of her mind, Mia heard the sounds, saw the lights—but they made no sense to her. Only escape mattered. Only escape made sense. Taking in a loud intake of breath, she opened her mouth and let out the most unholy scream she would ever remember hearing. Derek actually hesitated in the face of it, then twisted her around to face him and drew his fist back. She squeezed her eyes shut and heard the impact of flesh on bone, the agonizing groan of incomprehensible pain registering on all sensors.

When she opened her eyes, she saw Jack—an aluminum baseball bat in his hands— standing over Derek's twitching body on the ground. He turned to her and she fell into his arms. Every one of the stings and welts and gashes she'd fought to ignore all night long finally came together in a cacophonic symphony of agony to tell her in no uncertain terms—she was alive.

16

Life got boring.

Jack leaned over Mia's sleeping form in his bed and watched her face. Her eyes were blinking rapidly behind her eyelids. She was dreaming. He brushed a long tendril of dark hair from her face and she stirred. She must have been on the verge of awakening. He loved seeing her like this. *About as vulnerable as this girl can get.*

Unless you count that terrible night eight weeks ago when she fell into his arms, naked from the waist up, her hands tied behind her back, sobbing like he'd never seen her do and quivering in his arms.

He'd never forget the race down I-75, flanked by police cruisers, sirens blaring, growing ever closer to the dot that had stopped on the GPS map. All the while knowing that a stopped dot meant something else was happening. How had they found her in time? He knew he owed God massive time on his knees for that one. That, and a stubborn woman named Mia intent on breaking all the rules and scribbling in the margins.

Thank God.

He leaned over and kissed Mia's full lips and she languidly opened her eyes and smiled at him.

"Perv," she whispered around her smile.

"I'll show you perv," he said, slipping into bed with her and drawing her body against his. He cupped her bottom with both hands and felt her throaty laugh as if it was coming from inside him.

"No time, dear boy," she said, her eyes closed again. She stretched in his arms and yawned. "Work to do."

"You are indefatigable," he said, kissing her mouth again.

"I was just going to say the same thing about you."

"I think we have time," he said, squeezing her bottom. But she pulled away.

"That's just it, Jack," she said, sitting up in bed and stretching again. "We have all the time in the world. *After* we finish out work."

In the two months since Mia's abduction, she had become more determined than ever to find Victoria's killer—and that meant going through all the guys on the list one by one. In some ways, crazy Derek's attack had reinvigorated Mia's determination to find the real killer —as if she'd needed more reasons.

Although Derek had begun ranting as soon as he'd roused from the bash across the temple Jack gave him the night he kidnapped Mia, some of what he said made sense. In his fevered mind, the woman who'd spurned him—Vickie—had become famous beyond anyone's expectations. Even though that fame had happened posthumously, in Derek's addled, revenged-soaked thinking it was fame he could, unfairly, never hope to achieve. One thing he knew for sure, though, was that Victoria's infamy—deserved or not—was created by a celebrity-focused media frenzy. And because Mia led him to believe she was a reporter, for him the face of that media was Mia Kazmaroff.

Unfortunately, while Derek was sitting in jail on charges of kidnapping and murder—both of which would surely send him to prison for life—his DNA evidence for Victoria's murder didn't match.

Jack watched Mia as she ran a comb through her long hair then bent to look under the bed for her clothes. It didn't matter. One case solved. One killer off the streets.

Now if only Mia felt that way, too.

"We still going to your mom's for dinner tonight?" he asked as she pulled on shoes and socks. Their brief moment of afternoon delight after a late lunch had turned into an impromptu—and much needed—nap for Mia. For that Jack was glad. Lately, she pushed herself too far and too long.

"Yep," she said. "She's totally stressed over the whole wedding thing. I swear, they should just run off somewhere."

"She's doing it for you."

"That's crazy. Why does she think I want her to have a big wedding?"

"It's not really that big."

"It's bigger than a Justice of the Peace and brunch at Cracker Barrel."

"That's true."

She came and sat down on the bed next to him. "I've got two guys today. Both in Riverside."

"Kind of a trek on a Friday," Jack said. "What with rush hour and all."

"I know, but once they're done, we can focus on Midtown for the next month. Won't that be convenient?"

He kissed her. "So convenient."

"Can we run by Wojinziky's while we're at it? Pretty please?"

Jack frowned. While Mia had filled in the details of her day before Derek nabbed her, he still didn't like the whole Wojinziky element to this fixation of hers.

"Is there a reason? I thought you said he's been going nowhere and doing nothing."

"I know. He has. I just want to do a boots-on-the-ground surveillance. I read in a blog post for PIs that it's better to layer your surveillance methods."

He sighed and ran a hand through his hair. Before he could answer, Mia spoke up.

"Never mind," she said, softly. "I can track him from the computer. There's no reason to go to his place."

No reason except Mia could not unstick from her belief that Jeff Wojinziky was Victoria's killer. Even to the point of befriending Wojinziky's ex-fiancée.

"No," he said, squeezing her arm. "We'll go if you want. Talk to his ex-fiancée recently?"

"Not since last week. She's still hooked on him."

"She tell you yet why she broke up with him?"

"No. She says it would be a betrayal."

"Sounds ominous."

*****

Mia was happy to let Jack drive to her mother's house at the end of their afternoon of interviews. After the work he did on a daily basis to keep her spirits up and pretend to care about the Victoria case, it was the least she could do. Even Ned was bored with hearing about the case. And of course, the chief shut down if she even hinted she might bring it up.

Was it time to let it go? To admit defeat and pick up the banner of a life with this one significant failure hanging over it? Was it that time yet?

One by one, the suspects—the ones she'd been so sure of—had been cleared and fallen to the wayside. Who killed Victoria? Not Joshua Cook. He had an ironclad for the time of death. Not Derek, his DNA was nowhere it needed to be to pin it on him. Not Cargill. His wife loathed him enough to clean his clock in the divorce, but confirmed that her husband had been with her that night. That only left Nathan Turner—whose alibi and DNA were both MIA—and Jeff Wojinziky.

Mia held Daisy on her lap and let her out the window as they drove to Jess's neighborhood. When they got within a mile, Daisy would start to whine. Somehow the little dog always knew when they were close.

How did Mia know it was Wojinziky? Did it matter? She *knew* it. His guilt was as sure and infallible in her mind as DNA in a laboratory.

Yet he walked free and the Atlanta Major Crimes division allowed the days to pass, nudging Victoria's case further and further into the deep freeze of cold cases. Was anybody even working it anymore?

She turned to look at Jack as he concentrated on the road. Her heart soared to see his face, serious and handsome. His eyes a cerulean blue that missed nothing.

"We need someone on the force to feed us inside information," she said.

He laughed and glanced at her. "Yeah, that'd be helpful."

"I'm serious."

"Okay. You know it's not me, right? Half the guys on the force hated me. They think I'm a stooge for going private."

Mia sighed. "I thought we had the chief."

"He was pretty responsive that time I called him to say I thought you were in trouble," Jack reminded her.

"Yeah, yeah."

"He's done that on more than one occasion as a matter of fact."

"He has to. How would he explain it to his fiancée if you called in an SOS on me and he didn't respond?"

"The chief didn't do it for Jess's sake, Mia." Jack's tone was admonishing.

"I just don't understand why—if his people aren't going to bust their ass to solve Victoria's case—he doesn't let *me* do it."

"I'll bet you do understand."

"Oh, whatever."

As they pulled into Jess's neighborhood, Mia put her hand on Jack's arm.

"I haven't thanked you for helping me with this case," she said. "Even though I know you think it's a colossal waste of time."

"I don't think that."

"Well, anyway, thank you. I'm so glad nobody punched you today."

"Bright start to my weekend." He grinned that grin that made her insides melt, and for a moment Victoria and Tracy and Mindy and the chief and everybody else who created turmoil and snagged major portions of her thoughts faded away.

"I love you, Jack."

"I love you, too, Mia."

Daisy began to whine.

*****

The evening with Jess was relaxed and easy-going. It occurred to Jack at one point that part of that might be because Maxwell wasn't there. He'd had to work late. Even Jess seemed more at ease. Jack and Mia had been so busy in the last few months, between Mia's obsession with the Internet Hussy case and Jack's cooking business, plus they'd picked up a few cheating spouse cases. It was a surprise how quickly the wedding had snuck up on all of them.

Jack and Jess made a basic *spaghetti alla carbonara*, one of Mia's favorites. Since it was just the three of them, they opted to eat in the kitchen—another reason things felt so relaxed. As Jess brought the garlic bread to the table and Mia poured the wine, Jack dished up.

"Oh, tell my mom about the one guy we interviewed tonight," Mia said.

"Which one?" Jack set her dish in front of her.

"You know. The guy who was ginormous."

Jack turned to Jess, who was listening expectantly, her face upturned, a smile on her lips. It always surprised Jack how young Jess looked. She had to be late-fifties and he knew she'd never had any work done. He also knew she'd suffered terrible loss and pain. But her brow remained uncreased.

"There was just no way he was a candidate," Jack said, "and so as soon as he answered the door, I started to backpedal. You know, like, 'So sorry, there's been a mistake...'"

"And I could tell Jack was about to close things down—" Mia said.

"So she leans past me and grabs the guy by the arm!"

"Goodness, Mia, dear," Jess said, her hand to her mouth. "Was that wise?"

"And then Mia shrieks," Jack said. "And trust me, usually during these interviews, it's not Mia shrieking. It's either the guy who's being ambushed or me after the guy decides to deck me as a result of being ambushed."

Mia put the wine bottle down with a thump and looked at her mother.

"His arm came off in my hand," she said. "I'm standing there with this…this plastic thing with fingers and the guy's standing there…"

"And then your daughter gets the giggles," Jack said, frowning at Mia and shaking his head, as Jess burst out laughing. "Oh, I see it runs in the family," he said, still shaking his head but smiling too.

"I trust you didn't pick up anything useful from the poor man's prosthetic?" Jess said, still laughing.

"Not so much," Mia said, seating herself. "Oh, I hear Daisy outside. Y'all carry on. Let me get her." She jumped up and ran through the living room to the French doors leading outside.

Jess touched Jack on the wrist.

"Are there any signs she's giving up on this case?" she asked, all traces of mirth gone now.

"You know your daughter better than that. No. She'll be working it from the nursing home."

"I'm picking up on a little something…flat from her."

"I'm not surprised. We don't have any leads and nothing is moving forward."

"But these men you're interviewing…"

"We're just eliminating them. But yeah, what happens when we get to the last of them if, dear God, we ever do get to the last of them, and she hasn't found him? What then?"

Mia came back in.

"Hey, you guys are looking serious again. What happened? The chief call or something?"

"Enough of that. He's under a lot of stress," Jess said, focusing on her plate. "The wedding is in a week, you know."

"Wow. I knew it was creeping up," Mia said.

Jess smiled at her. "You make it sound like an exotic animal or a plague."

"I'm sure you'll both be glad when it's behind you," Jack said, watching Jess's face.

"It has been more stress than I expected," Jess admitted. "Oh, my, this *carbonara* is wonderful, Jack."

"Well, we both did it."

"Teaming up with Jack," Mia said around her first forkful of spaghetti. "I highly recommend it."

The rest of the dinner was pleasant and light. But between Mia's low-grade depression about how nothing was happening on the Victoria Baskerville case and Jess's worry and strain over her upcoming nuptials, Jack felt like he was sandwiched between a very edgy rock and a fairly sticky hard place.

Hopefully, things would calm down after the wedding was behind them. Jack had no doubt Maxwell adored Jess. But whatever was going on with his daughter, Mindy, was seriously polluting the pleasure of that adoration. Anyone with eyes could see that.

Jess took Daisy and curled up on the couch while Mia and Jack tackled the dishes. It wasn't unusual for a chef to enjoy every aspect of the cooking process—even the washing up. He liked the feeling of the hot water, the aroma of the soap and the sensation of getting the dishes squeaky clean, rinsed and stacked. It was a circle and, for him, it wasn't complete until the dishes were put away and the leftovers tucked into plastic lidded containers.

Mia dried and hummed—which was how Jack knew that, just for now and just for a few minutes, she was at peace.

"I can't believe the wedding's coming up so soon," she said, stacking a dish. "I feel guilty I wasn't more help."

"I guess you mean *any* help."

She snapped him with her dishtowel and reached for another dish from the rack where he was placing them.

"Which reminds me," he said, giving her shoulder a light squeeze. "I'll be right back."

"You better be," Mia said, continuing to hum again.

Jack went into the living room where Jess was relaxing.

"Jess, did you ever find out if anyone coming to the rehearsal dinner has any allergies?"

"Oh, thank you for reminding me. Bill's uncle Joe has a problem with peanuts. Will that be okay?"

Jack frowned and looked around the living room.

"It should be okay. Mind if I use your computer to double-check the recipe for the sea bass?" He sat down and typed in "Daisy" and the browser opened up.

"Damn, Jess, you've got about a hundred unopened emails here. Do you ever use this machine?"

"No. I'm not clever that way. I do everything by phone."

Jack noticed the subject line of one of the unread emails that read *Maxwell Wedding*. He opened it, a feeling of dread inching up his spine at the first line of the email: *Are you sure you want to cancel?*

It was dated five weeks ago.

"Jess, did you cancel the catering for the wedding?" He clicked on another email. "Or the flowers? Or the reception hall?"

Jess got up from the couch to come look over his shoulder. "I don't use email," she said. "I talked to all those people by phone."

Jack drilled down into the history. "Yeah, but…they were all cancelled from your computer," he said. "Over a month ago."

*****

The next morning, Mia sat at a table in her local coffee shop. While not addicted to coffee as Jack clearly was, Mia had to admit few places smelled as pleasant as a Starbucks. That wasn't the main reason she'd arranged to meet Mindy here, but one thing she knew about computer nerds—they were all speed junkies in one form or another.

And in Mia's experience, you wanted to make your mark as comfortable as possible before you slammed the trap shut.

Not surprisingly, Mindy was thirty minutes late. Mia waved to her when she saw her enter the shop. Mindy's eyes darted around the shop interior as if she expected a plant of CIA informants hiding behind every opened newspaper.

Even from fifteen feet away, she looked like a basket case.

It hadn't been difficult to get her to meet. The woman was intensely curious.

Another characteristic of the typical computer hacker.

Thank you, Mindy, for being such a helpful stereotype.

Mia crossed her arms and waited for Mindy to make her way across the coffee shop to her table. She'd ordered an espresso for Mindy but it had long gone cold.

It hadn't taken Mia and Jack five minutes to find the remote access app on Jess's computer. Mindy hadn't even bothered to remove the thumb drive or hide the fact that it had been installed the very day Mindy and her mother had visited Jess. With only six days until the wedding, the sabotage had thrown Mia's usually calm and balanced mother into a flurry of tears and hysteria.

And for that, Mia was not feeling very forgiving.

"Wow, I have to admit you have some pretty serious computer skills," Mia said as Mindy slumped into the chair opposite her. She was wearing jeans, strategically ripped at the knees, and an old cardigan with the elbows worn and frayed. There was a definite Dragon Tattoo-feel about Mindy that was compelling for its eccentricity.

"All that computer cognitive genius," she said. "Must come in handy changing diapers."

Mindy leaned back in her chair. "What do you want?"

"I want you to leave my mother alone. The wedding's still going on in spite of you— the only difference is now you won't be there." Mia slid the thumb drive across the table to her.

"You're lying," Mindy said. "My father would never get married without me." She picked up the small plastic drive. "Does he know?"

"That you put illegal software on my mom's computer and cancelled all her appointments for the wedding? No. Because she insisted Jack and I not tell him. Seems she has this fantasy about all of us being a family some day."

"Dad did say insanity ran in your family."

"I'm just sorry you didn't get an earful of some really heavy sexting between the two of them."

"Are we done?"

"Don't you have a husband? And a kid?"

"I have a very full life. What's your point?"

"Does your husband know you're doing this shit?"

"That's none of your business."

"I read online that most hackers are driven by an insatiable curiosity to see how things work. Must be frustrating being just a boring old Dunwoody housewife."

"You're nuts. In fact, Dad tells me on a regular basis how nuts you are."

"That's not news. Oh, but this might be." Mia leaned over the table until her face was near Mindy's. "I love your Dad. How's that feel?"

"Shut up!" Mindy sat up straight in her chair. "Shut up about him."

"Yeah, I thought that'd hit a nerve. Truth is he's like my own Pop-Pop the way he listens to me and gives me advice all the time—"

"You're lying! He says you're crazy!"

"You already played that card, Mindy. It's actually a shtick between your dad and me about how crazy he thinks I am...in a totally lovable way, of course."

"That's not true. He told me you were a pain in the ass."

"Same as with you, right? I mean, you've got this gift for computers and I know the chief. He must hate that."

"You don't know him at all."

"But I'm right about this, aren't I? Does he love the fact that you're a hacker?"

Mindy hesitated. "Don't be ridiculous. Hacking is illegal."

"It is, isn't it? Pretty inconvenient to have the one thing you do best in the world be the one thing your father detests."

Mindy glowered at her.

"I mean," Mia said, "stands to reason—he doesn't understand computers so he doesn't understand *you*. Major disconnect."

"You don't know what you're talking about."

"I know I'd like to offer you a job."

Mindy's mouth fell open. It was clear she couldn't think of a single response to that.

"Think about it," Mia continued. "Jack and I could use a major league hacker—for those times we can't always play by the book—and having someone in the family who can do it would be extremely helpful."

Mindy flushed and jumped up from her chair.

"Dad was right, you're totally nuts. And I'm done here. So tell, me," she said snidely, "is it going to be a living room wedding in that dark cave of a dump your mom calls home? Since the minister got cancelled, will there be a hippy throwing flowers in the air and declaring a common law marriage is just as binding? Will there be Kool-Aid for the guests or is that only for my father?"

"You can't stop it from happening," Mia said laughing. "He's. Marrying. Her. Welcome to the family, you psycho."

"We'll just see." She turned and stomped away.

17

Jess Kazmaroff's wedding day was a bright, cool spring day with all of Atlanta's floral show in full bloom. Jack carried an armful of white roses into the church. With the cancellation of all of the wedding florist orders, he and Mia had amassed a collection from various florists nearby.

He had a box of fliers he'd created that morning, which would be handed out after the ceremony alerting all guests to the change in venue for the reception.

Mia hadn't said what happened in her showdown with Mindy and the scramble to fill in the cancelled appointments, photographer, and catering had kept Ned, Mia and Jack running for four days. In a way, the wedding felt a lot more personal now. Instead of the Cancun honeymoon—the flights for which were cancelled weeks ago—Jess arranged for them to drive up to Brasstown Bald. When she told Maxwell she preferred a cabin in the North Georgia mountains where she could take walks and have him teach her to fly fish, the big lug nearly cried.

Jack set the flowers down and looked around. It was two hours before aisle-walking time. Ned came out of an anteroom, an SLR camera in his hands.

"Hey, Jack, any more flowers in the back of your car?"

"No, this is it. Did the new photographer cancel?"

Ned hefted the camera. "This one we can't put on Maxwell's crazy daughter," he said. "He got the flu."

"Terrific."

"Did you deliver the cake to the reception hall?"

When the reception venue was cancelled Jack arranged to have everything moved to the VFW Hall in Norcross. In fact, the only thing that hadn't gotten totally screwed by Mindy's sabotage was the church, itself. Because Jess saw and spoke to her priest weekly, when he got the email canceling her church date, he simply ignored it.

"Yeah, Mia delivered it."

"Surprised you trusted her with your masterpiece."

"I'm trying. Have you seen the chief?"

"He's in one of the dressing rooms trying not to look like he's coming apart at the seams."

"That's only because he's smart enough to worry Jess might come to her senses."

They walked to the front of the church.

"Haven't spoken to Mia in awhile," Ned said. "She doing okay?"

Jack shrugged. "She's still pretty focused on the Internet Hussy case."

"You mean obsessed."

"Yeah, that's what I mean."

"That's a dead end, isn't it? I mean, nobody has any leads?"

Jack sighed. "Yeah, but the worst of it, because it's an open case, is she can't have access to any evidence the Atlanta detectives discover. And while it was great that she helped solve Tracey Kilpatrick's murder, it didn't budge the needle at all on Maxwell relenting on her working on Victoria's case."

"You need to do a better job of distracting her," Ned said, his hands on his hips.

"I thought that was your job."

Ned laughed. "Yeah, right. But speaking of jobs, I'm off to pick up Jess and her dress."

"Isn't Mia doing that after she delivers the cake?"

"There's only room in the car for the driver, the dress and the bride. I told Mia we'd meet her here." Ned looked at his watch and frowned. "I'd better get going." He slapped Jack on the shoulder and trotted down the aisle to the exit. As he opened the front door, Mindy Payne stepped into the church and was momentarily backlit. She hesitated, then turned slowly, as if aware she was being watched.

Jack approached her. "Looking for your dad?"

"Eventually," Mindy said. She wore jeans and flip-flops and carried a long garment bag, presumably containing her bridesmaid's dress. "I'm in charge of the entertainment." She smiled and looked past Jack. "I need to find where the church AV room is located."

"I have no idea, but the chief's in the last dressing room off the narthex and down that hall."

"No problem," she said, sweetly. "I'm sure I'll find it."

Jack watched her walk down the hall and his gut tightened. She was way too happy today of all days for that to be good for anyone.

*****

Mindy dumped her dress on a chair in the parish AV room. She'd called ahead and discovered they only had an LCD projector with a ten by twelve foot screen.

Archaic. But it would do.

Just in case there was a more updated way of showing the video at the reception—assuming everyone made it that far which was not at all certain—she had the video as a QuickTime file on a jump drive too.

Otherwise how's it going to go viral from a stupid church projector?

She stooped to examine the power amplifier system on a cart in the corner. The video was pure gold all on its own of course, but if there was any way she could get the audio to link up for the full effect of "Jess's" cries of delight, Mindy would be thanking the AV gods forever. *Is that blasphemous?* she thought, with a grin.

"I thought I saw you come in."

She whirled around to face her father walking into the room.

"Getting the video ready?" he asked, looking past her. He already had his suit on. It had been a long time since Mindy had seen him so dressed up—his last wife's funeral came to mind.

"That's, right," she said. "Just doing some sound checks so there are no hiccups."

"I wanted to tell you, Mindy, how grateful I am that you're doing this. I know this has been hard for you."

"It's okay, Dad. As long as you're happy."

He looked nervous, which surprised her. Bill Maxwell was a rock. To see him now, jittery and ruffled was disconcerting.

"I want you to get to know Jess," he said. "I guess because I love her—and I love you—it's hard for me to…to see why you can't be friends."

"Sure," she said. She felt something cold and hard seize up inside her chest. "I know you want that. Stands to reason you would."

"I wish you could understand." He watched her, his eyes liquid and sad. Mindy held herself together, not moving, not speaking, not breathing—hoping he would just leave.

"Okay," she said, her voice a squeak.

"I know we never talked about it...why I left. And I'm sorry about that." He nodded as if he'd delivered sage, important advice and then turned to walk out the door.

The pain and the hurt wouldn't be contained another moment. Not with her father crowbarring the lid off her carefully packed box of resentment.

"You left me alone with her," she said in a small voice.

He stopped and turned around. "Your mother?"

"You left her because she was a drunk and self-destructive. I get it. Only she got worse when you left. And there was only me to pick up the mangled, ugly, bloody pieces. *You* let that happen. You *made* that happen. But you didn't watch it happen."

He opened his mouth, his eyes moving around the room.

"I just...I wanted out so bad," he said, his eyes finally resting on her, "that I didn't think how it would be for you. I am so sorry for that. My God, I am so sorry, Mindy."

"It felt like you left me too, Dad."

He reached for her. "I'll never leave you, darling girl. I swear on all that is holy, you'll be the one out of all of them, I know that for sure, who I'll never leave."

Mindy felt her shoulders sag beneath his pressing fingers. He wouldn't let her look away. For a split second, she remembered him from so many years ago.

Those same eyes of love: reading to her, throwing the ball to her, laughing with her.

"Do you hear me, Mindy?" he said, giving her a little shake. "This isn't like that time. This time I'm not leaving you. I'm bringing you with me. Do you understand?"

Her eyes drilled into his, searching. She wanted to answer him. The lump in her throat was burning and she felt tears stinging her eyes.

"Jess and Mia are standing by, too," he said, "They want you. They want both of us."

She shook her head to chase the tears away. Trying to sound flippant, she said, "Taking applications to form a family?"

"You've met Mia. You know she's no BS."

"I know she's crazy."

"So the two of you should get along great."

Mindy smiled in spite of herself. He brought her into his arms and hugged her tight.

"What a zoo it's going to be at family holidays," she whispered into his chest.

"I can't wait," he said. He pulled back to look at her again. "And get a load of this—your mom's welcome too."

She nodded and wiped her tears away. "Okay, Dad. Well, it's a new angle, that's for sure."

"See if you can work it, sugar," he said, moving a tendril of her hair from her eyes. "I really need you to. I think *you* really need you to, too."

She stood on tiptoe and kissed him, then let out a long breath. "Think Jess will forgive me?"

"She already has."

"All right then. It's your special day, Dad. Let's do this thing."

The first strains of the wedding march began, faltered and then stopped. Her father looked away as if he'd been goosed. For a moment, his face looked panicked.

"Are you sure you're going to be okay?" he asked, but his gaze was on the door.

She laughed. "I could ask you the same thing."

"I'll be fine," he said, looking back at her. "Now that I've got you and Jess, I'll be more than fine."

"I need to hit the ladies' room to do some damage control," she said, pointing to her streaked mascara.

"Don't take too long. I need you next to me when I do this."

"I'll be there," she said. He turned and walked out of the room. She stood quietly for a moment, still feeling the pressure of his hands on her shoulders. There were more people walking up and down the hallway now. She glanced at her watch. Less than an hour away. She turned back to the projector and found the USB port on the side. The thumb drive went in easily and she felt a rush of intoxication.

Yep. This was definitely going to be a very special day.

*****

Mia sped toward the church. It wasn't that she was late exactly, but she hadn't meant to take so much time at the reception venue.

Jack will thank me when I tell him how they were about to put his caprese salad in the refrigerator. The parking lot had filled up. Glancing at the digital clock on her dashboard, she realized she was later than she thought.

She took a long breath to steady herself. All she really had to do was get into her bridesmaid's dress, put her hair into a ponytail or something and borrow some blush and mascara from her mother.

Her mother.

In the scramble to replace all the things necessary to have the wedding come off on time, Mia hadn't had much time to spend with Jess. A hurried phone conversation this morning and a brief handoff last night was about it. She would make it up to her. After all, wasn't everything she was doing now for Jess?

Mia yanked the garment bag that contained her dress out of the backseat of the car. In fact, twenty minutes before launch gave her plenty of time to dress, have a heart-to-heart with Jess and still be in place next to the chief when Jess was escorted down the aisle by Ned.

Locking her car, she hurried across the parking lot, scanning it for anyone she knew, but knowing they were probably all already inside—Jack, Ned, her mother, the chief. Would Mindy show? It didn't matter. Short of stuffing a roman candle in the pipe organ, she couldn't stop if from happening now.

An usher stood at the door, welcoming people as they came in. Mia slipped in among a throng of entering guests—none of whom she knew—and stood in the narthex to get her bearing. Holy Family Catholic Church had been their family parish for as long as Mia could remember, and although Mia had stopped going years ago, Jess was as involved as ever.

Mia shouldn't have been so surprised to see the number of people who had come to watch Jess get married. This was Jess's church, and Jess's people. Mia squeezed past a group of four well-dressed middle-aged couples waiting to be shown to their seats and was about to run down the north hall to the dressing rooms when she saw something that made her stop.

A sudden coldness fluttered through her chest.

It was impossible. He can't be here.

But he was. He stood by the water fountain, arms crossed, eyes dull and spiritless, waiting for the usher to lead him to his place.

Jeff Wojinziky.

18

The music started and stopped twice. It reminded Jess of what happens during intermission at musicals when they want everyone to put down their drinks and come back to their theatre seats for part two of the show.

Part two of my life.

From where Jess sat in the bride's dressing room, she could see a portion of the parking lot through the window. The minute she spotted Mia's blue Toyota whipping into a parking spot, Jess felt herself relax. She just needed fifteen minutes—no, make that five. Five minutes to hold her dear girl—the only person left in their loving family of four—to remind her that today only changed things for the better. It wasn't a speech, exactly, but she'd put some thought into what to say. There just hadn't been a moment before now to say it.

The music started again and stopped. Was whoever was operating the sound system attempting to corral guests into their seats? Fact was, it was more than a little irritating. Jess stood and walked to the full-length mirror in the room.

The gown was beautiful. The beadwork and sequins looked like pixie dust sprinkled against a background of pale tea-colored satin. Jess sparkled when she moved.

Not at all like I felt the first time I did this. I got married in a simple dress. I knew nothing then. Except the caliber of the man I was to marry. She smiled in memory. *That hasn't changed. I knew it then, I know it now. The only difference was I was alone forty years ago when Gaspar and I wed. And today I have our Mia.*

She walked to the door and peered down the hall. *Surely Mia knows to come to me? Where was she?* Mindy emerged at the end of the hall, her gown bag over her shoulder.

"Mindy, dear," Jess called to her. "Have you seen Mia?"

Mindy made a face and Jess felt her heart sink. She'd hoped that her soon-to-be stepdaughter had come around to Jess marrying her father.

"Well, if you see her, please tell her I'd like a word."

Mindy walked past without answering, which Jess thought was at least an improvement over a snide comment. She sighed and closed the door.

Why do I feel sad today? Why do I feel like something bad is about to happen?

She went back to the mirror and looked at herself. All she could see was the beautiful dress and a perfectly miserable middle-aged woman.

A sharp rap on the door made her jump and she hurried to it and pulled it open. Ned stood there, smiling, expectant.

"You ready?" he asked.

"So soon? Is it really time?"

"We have a few minutes. You okay, Mrs. K?" He frowned and stepped into the room.

"Have you seen Mia? I know she's in the church. I saw her drive up."

"Want me to track her down?"

"No. I just wanted to have a word. It doesn't matter."

The music started up again. Ned grinned.

"Look like they're giving everyone plenty of warning, huh?" he said.

"I *hope* it's plenty of warning."

Ned took her arm and tucked it under his and patted her hand. "Don't worry, Mrs. K," he said. "She'll be here."

*****

What in the hell is Jeff Wojinziky doing at my mother's wedding?

Mia pushed through the crowd of people, her heart pounding in her throat. *Did Mom know him? Is Maxwell related to him?*

The closer she got, the more obvious it was that Wojinziky did not want to be where he was. He leaned against the wall nearest the portal to the church as if waiting impatiently for someone. Surely, he hadn't come alone. Did he bring his wife?

The minute she was close to him, Mia tossed her dress bag over her shoulder to free up both hands and grabbed him around the waist. He immediately jerked away but she hung on. He swung around to face his attacker and she loosened her hold to latch onto one of his hands. He was a big man and the moment of surprise was receding quickly. He flung her away from him, making her fall backward into an elderly couple standing near.

Mia gasped and fought to keep her feet as the couple squawked and scurried away. Her purse and dress bag slid to the floor.

"What the hell, you crazy bitch!" Wojinziky said, staring at her—but also looking around as if worried someone had seen him. He rubbed his arms where she'd grabbed him. He looked like he was trying to rub away the memory of the feel of her hands.

The crowd fell away in her vision and it was only him. He glared at her, then turned and plunged down one of the halls.

The agony of her discovery crept up her back like a raging sore, obliterating all sound and thought. She looked down at her hands and saw they were shaking. What she had felt, what she had experienced when she finally touched him, was anger and hurt and bone-deep disappointment. The kind of disappointment that defies any one occasion or moment in time but lasts and lasts, an indelible feature of your life, your very nature.

But he wasn't a killer.

Someone next to Mia tapped her on the shoulder and when she turned—like a robot, not seeing or caring —they handed her the dropped garment bag and her purse. She heard them talking to her, but could make out nothing of what they said. She nodded in response and took the items and walked down the hallway toward the restroom.

The last five months of tracking him, looking for clues and leads, poring over the files, even the door-to-door visits with Jack—all of it had been for nothing. The one thing she knew for sure, the one premise she used as her bedrock—that Jeff Wojinziky had killed Victoria—was a fantasy.

She opened the door to the ladies restroom and went to the sink counter. Without pausing to look in the mirror or check to see who else was in the room, she dropped her purse on the counter and unzipped her garment bag. Her mind was a whirl of noise and colors —but none of it from the restroom or the real world.

Disappointment has a color. It's not just a feeling. And it's dark.

She stripped off her jeans and sweatshirt, leaving them in a pile on the floor and pulled the bridesmaid's dress out of the bag.

It didn't matter that the single biggest let down of her life so far was happening on her mother's wedding day. *Put it away, process it later. Maybe it's not as bad as it feels. Just don't be the reason this isn't the happiest day of Mom's life.*

Mia stepped into the dress and zipped it up. She kicked off her shoes onto the pile of discarded clothes and pulled the matching pumps from the bottom of the bag. When she stood up, she stared into the mirror.

With her pale face and windblown hair, she looked a little like a deranged serial killer herself.

The bathroom door swung open and Mindy walked in.

"You do know there's a bridesmaid's dressing room for that, right?" she said, shaking her head and pushing past Mia into one of the stalls. "Weirdo."

How could I have been so wrong? Every other interaction with him—the very air around him—had vibrated with the truth of the damage he'd done to Victoria. How can this stupid gift let me down like this? Yes, he was angry. Yes, he was violent. But he'd never taken a life.

She stared again at her hands as if they had betrayed her.

"You got toilet paper in there, girly?"

The voice brought Mia out of the depths of her dejection in the space of a heartbeat. She snapped her head up. That voice. A voice you'd never forget. A voice that would make dogs howl from two counties over—strident, scratchy and discordant.

"Fuck off, grandma," Mindy replied to the woman in the stall next to her. "A little privacy, if you don't mind."

Mia went to the remaining empty stall. She grabbed a roll of toilet paper and handed it under the partition to the woman. She held onto the roll until she felt the woman's fingers on hers.

"Well, are you going to let go or what?" the woman snarled.

Mia released the roll, then went back to the mirror and stared into it, waiting. Jeff's wife was in that stall. And Mia's fingers still burned from the brief contact she'd made with her.

The touch of a murderer.

The stall door opened and a middle-aged woman with auburn hair filled the doorway. The same woman who was at Tracy's funeral. Their eyes met in the reflection of the mirror.

Not Jeff's wife—Jeff's *mother*. Mia pulled her cell phone out of her purse and typed a quick text. The woman came to stand next to Mia, set her purse on the counter and turned the faucet on.

"You'd think you kids could give the texting a break for just one hour. You're all obsessed."

"And you old farts are just clueless about technology," Mia said in a tight voice, her eyes on the message she'd just sent.

The woman sputtered. "*What* did you say to me?"

"I know you," Mia said, turning to her. "You're Jeff's mother."

246

The woman stopped washing her hands and stared at Mia in the same way a Velociraptor observes its prey.

"You know my son?" she asked, her voice flat, her eyes cold.

"Oh, yeah," Mia said. "We're friends. *Good* friends."

A pinging sound from her phone made her look at the screen. It was a single-word response from Beth, Jeff's ex-fiancée.

<Yes :-(>

Mia looked at Jeff's mother, who was now reaching for her purse, her eyes boring into Mia. The message Mia had sent Beth was brief and to the point.

<The real reason you left Jeff was his crazy mother, wasn't it?>

*****

Mindy pulled her gown back down over her hips and touched the barely visible lump of the AV remote control wand that she'd tucked into her bra. She'd lucked out to find it in the AV room because it featured a volume control that would come in handy during those big "Jess" crescendo moments.

Now she just needed to practice a few innocent looks in the mirror for when it all went down. Not that her father would buy it for a minute. But it was worth a try. In Mindy's experience, confession might be good for the soul but it was fucked up in most other situations.

What were those two talking about out there? She needed Mia and the old lady to split so she could be alone, but they seemed to be bonding or something. God, that crazy Mia would talk to anyone. Mindy would have to rely on her usual set of perfectly adequate expressions of innocence—the ones that had served her well enough up to now. She gave her dress a final tug and checked her shoes to make sure no toilet paper stuck to them and opened the door.

Mia stood in profile at the sink. The old lady stood in front of Mindy's stall door.

She was holding a large gun.

And it was pointed at Mindy's head.

19

Tanya Wojinziky waved the large Colt .45 at Mindy.

"I knew you'd come," she said. "I knew you'd be here today. Stand over there by the other one. Try to leave and you're dead."

"Are you mad?" Mindy said, edging over to where Mia was standing by the counter. "There's a church full of people twenty yards away."

"Is that what you're counting on? Well, you can forget it. I'm not letting you get away again."

"This isn't Beth, Mrs. Wojinziky," Mia said. "Although, there is a vague resemblance."

"What the hell is going on?" Mindy said, repeatedly fingering her plain gold necklace. She turned to Mia. "She has a *gun*."

"I heard him talking to you on the phone, you slut," Tanya hissed. "I know you want to get your hooks into him."

"I do not know what you're talking about," Mindy said, her eyes wide and focused on the gun pointed at her.

Tanya flicked her eyes to Mia.

"I don't know you," she said. "But I know her." She cocked the gun with her free hand and then steadied her gun hand with it. "And I know I won't let her get my boy. If I have to die trying—"

"You mean like you prevented Victoria Baskerville from getting him?" Mia said. "Jeff really liked Victoria, didn't he?"

"She was a whore."

"What did he do? Finally stand up to you?"

"I told him he couldn't see her again but she had him blinded by lust. I had to step in. She used her carnal ways on him and he was *powerless*." Tanya's eyes flickered back to Mindy. "Just like this one."

Mia put a hand on Mindy's shoulder and softened her voice.

"Okay," she said. "I agree she's a raving whore dog, but think about it—if you go to jail for shooting her, there will be literally hundreds of women over at your house on a daily basis," Mia said. "They'll be sleeping in your bed, cooking with your pots—"

She swung the gun back to Mia.

"Shut up!"

Mia put her hands up. "Without you there, they'll be lining up to get their claws into Jeff. One right after another. Maybe two at once."

Tanya's eyes were bouncing around in manic imaginings of what that would look like. Unfortunately, she appeared to be worse as a result. Now she seemed intent on shooting every woman of marrying age—starting with Mia and Mindy.

"Mama? You in there? Wedding's about to start."

Tanya turned her head in the direction of Jeff's voice on the other side of the restroom door. Mia saw her moment and lurched forward and grabbed Tanya's wrist with one hand. She wrapped her fingers around the barrel of the gun with her other hand and pushed it against Tanya's thumb. Tanya yelped and dropped the weapon.

"Get the gun!" Mia rasped in a low voice to Mindy, as she grappled with Tanya's wrists. The woman wasn't young but she was heavy. And she was insane with fury.

Mindy snatched the gun and smashed it against the side of Tanya's head. The woman crumpled to the bathroom floor.

"Okay, there's that," Mia said. She looked from Tanya to Mindy—who was shaking her head, trying to negate what just happened.

"Is everything okay in there?" Jeff's voice boomed through the door and the doorknob rattled.

"Yes, sir," Mia said in a fake Southern accent, walking backward to the door, keeping an eye on Tanya. "We are just fine in here as long as no nosy fella comes busting in on us in our altogether."

Mindy, still holding the gun, stared at the body on the floor. Mia placed her ear against the door for a moment before straightening up.

"He's gone." She went to Tanya's purse on the floor. "Shit, she has another gun in here."

Mia glanced at Mindy, who was watching Tanya's slighting twitching body. She looked like she was about to hyperventilate. Mia took the gun from Mindy and placed it on the floor away from her.

"How does she know your mother?" Mindy asked, her voice flat, her eyes transfixed by the body.

"Good question." Mia opened up Tanya's wallet and pulled out a newspaper clipping. "Here we go. She saw the announcement in yesterday's paper."

She pulled a tattered First Holy Communion card out of the billfold. "Whoa. Check it out. She's carrying around Jeff's Holy Communion picture from thirty years ago from this parish."

Mindy knelt on the floor. Mia guessed it was because her knees were shaking so bad it was either sit down or fall down. She hoped she wouldn't have to give Mindy mouth-to-mouth.

"Are you okay? You're breathing funny."

"This parish?" Mindy said. "The parish we are currently sitting in at this moment?"

"It answers how she knew my mother."

Tanya moaned and lashed out an arm, connecting solidly with Mindy's face and knocking her backward against the sink pedestals. Mia dropped the purse and leaned her weight onto the woman's back but Tanya evaded the pressure point. She got one knee under her and threw Mia off.

"I'll kill you bitches," Tanya muttered, but her words were slurred. She shook her head to clear it. Mia grabbed the gun and knocked Tanya solidly on the head again. Tanya blinked once and then her eyes rolled back in her head and slowly closed. She fell backward.

"I have no idea what I'm doing," Mia said, sending the Colt skidding across the floor away from them. She stood and reached for her purse on the counter. "We need to wrap this up before one of us accidentally kills her." She started to punch in 911 but Mindy stood, grabbing the sink counter for support, and put her hand on the phone.

"Wait," she said. She held up a finger to indicate she needed a moment to collect herself. "Don't call them just yet."

Mia frowned but didn't complete the call. Suddenly, the wedding music began. Both Mia and Mindy turned their heads in the direction of the music.

This time the music didn't stop.

"Come on," Mindy said. "I have an idea. But we need to hurry."

*****

"Oh, shit." Jack saw Mia and Mindy before the rest of them at the front of the altar did, but he could tell—by the building collective gasps—when, row by row, the rest of the guests spotted them. The two women walked, arm in arm, down the aisle toward the front of the church where Jack, Maxwell, and Jess waited with the priest. The music had just ended.

Even from thirty feet, he could see Mindy's left eye was swollen shut and Mia had a fat, bloody lip. They'd clearly made some attempt to straighten hair that looked like it had been caught in a category five hurricane and clean up the matching bridesmaids' dresses speckled with blood, dirt and, in Mia's case, a rip to her thigh.

"I'm going to kill both of them," Maxwell said under his breath, but Jack saw Jess's fingers tighten around the chief's arm.

"They're here," she said softly. "And they're together."

When they got closer, amazingly, Jack saw that Mia was smiling.

"Time enough later to hear their story," Jess said, as Mindy and Mia took their places on either side of Maxwell and Jess. Mia reached out and squeezed her mother's hand and Mindy gave her father the most angelic look Jack had ever witnessed this side of heaven.

Oh, this was going to be good.

It was a beautiful ceremony and went off without a stumble, a fumbled line or missed cue. When Maxwell and Jess turned to face the applause of their guests as Mr. and Mrs. William Maxwell, Mia took Jack's arm and fell into place beside him for the promenade down the aisle. Ned appeared from the front row and held his arm out to Mindy to escort her.

"What the hell happened?" Jack whispered to Mia as they walked behind the newlyweds.

"Before I get into that, you might want to tell the chief to get somebody here from downtown," Mia said, nodding and smiling benignly at the wedding guests on either side of the aisle. "Mindy and I caught Victoria Baskerville's killer in the ladies room."

Jack nearly stumbled and Mia gripped his arm.

"We've got her tied up with choir robe cords in the closet of the bridesmaids' room."

"It's a *woman*?" Jack choked out.

"Just tell the chief, okay?" Mia said sweetly. "And then let's put it aside for one day, shall we? I intend to celebrate my mother's happy day to the hilt."

They stopped at the end of the church where Jess, the chief, Mindy and Ned were huddled before the church entrance.

Maxwell was frowning at his daughter.

"But I thought you said there was supposed to be a movie *before* the ceremony?"

"Technical difficulties, Dad. Sorry about that."

"Well, show it at the reception then. Might be better there anyway."

"Sure, Dad," Mindy said. "If I can work out the kinks."

*****

The VFW hall was bare bones, anchored by a massive American flag at the end of one wall and strung with limp paper streamers. Mia was sure they must have been there since the last Veterans Day party. It didn't matter. There was a sound system—and it was a good one—hooked up to someone's music library, a decent kitchen where Jack had overseen the wedding lunch, and plenty of tables and chairs surrounding a good-sized dance floor.

All in all, very satisfactory Mia thought as she surveyed the scene from the kitchen entrance. Most people were either on the dance floor or eating cake. Mindy stood next to Mia sipping a glass of champagne.

"Too bad you couldn't get the video to work," Mia said dryly. "I'm sure our parents would've enjoyed it."

"Yeah, well," Mindy said, "you know technology. You can never trust it."

"Is that your husband over there waving to you?"

Mindy looked in the direction of a handsome man with a small girl in his arms.

"Bethany's probably whining," Mindy said, finishing off her drink.

"I know how she feels," Mia said. "My feet are killing me."

Mindy gave her a sidelong look. "You made me a kind of hero in my old man's eyes today. That's a new feeling for me."

"You *were* a kind of hero today. Knocking old ladies out with gun butts then realizing that calling the cops *before* the wedding would seriously ruin the chief and Jess's day."

"Yeah, yeah."

"No, really," Mia said. "That was good thinking."

Mindy picked up her clutch purse and brushed what looked like crumbs off her dress. It was blood spatter.

"By the way," she said, "that job offer you made to me at the coffee shop a couple days ago?"

"What about it?"

"I accept."

Mia looked at Mindy and they both smiled.

"I kind of thought you might."

Mindy walked across the room of wedding guests to meet her husband. He flashed Mia a grin and then wrapped his free arm around Mindy to shepherd her out of the reception hall. *He looks like a nice guy. That's good. I'm glad she's got somebody like that.*

"Leave it to you to turn your mother's wedding into a crime scene," Jack said as he came up from behind Mia and kissed her on the neck. He'd loosened his tie and his face was relaxed and cheerful.

"Hi, handsome. You look happy."

"Murray just called."

"The civil suit?"

He nodded. "They dropped it."

"Oh, Jack!"

"I know. Great news."

Mia turned her gaze back to the dance floor, her heart swelling. Maxwell and Jess were still dancing in the crowded hall. Jess's gown was beautiful as it dusted the floor with her languid movements. Even with the last-minute booking of the reception hall at the VFW, it was hard to see how Jess could look any happier than she did at this moment.

Could the day be any more perfect?

"Is the chief speaking to me yet?" she asked.

"Don't worry about him," Jack said. "You solved the case of the Internet Hussy, after all. Pretty nice wedding gift in my mind. *And* you brought his daughter back into the fold. Although I'm not sure Maxwell is thrilled with how all *that* went down."

"I can't believe I was wrong about Jeff," Mia said, turning back to Jack. "I got my wires crossed somehow. And I was so sure."

"Where did he go by the way? I didn't see him."

"He sat through the whole service with an empty seat next to him. When the cops showed up, I didn't see him again. Probably went to go call Beth now that Crazy Mama is out of the picture."

"Had you even met his mother before today?"

"No. I'd heard her voice, and we both saw her at Tracy's funeral, but I didn't know it was her."

"Why was she at the funeral?"

"Because of the connection to Victoria. She wasn't absolutely sure Jeffy-boy wasn't somehow involved with the twins. Fact is, if Derek hadn't killed Tracy, Tanya Wojinziky probably would have."

"Nut case."

"Totally."

"You ready to finally close this case, partner?"

Mia put her hand on his arm. Her eyes were soft and glowing. "You have been so supportive during all this, Jack. No matter what I asked of you, you were right there for me—even when I was being stuffed in trunks and strange men were throwing punches at you. Thank you."

"It's in the manual," he said, shrugging. "Chapter One: What Men Must Do for the Women They Love."

"I like that manual." She slipped her arm in his and laid her head on his shoulder. "Take me home, Jack. We need to add a new chapter to it."

"I hope it's steamy."

"Oh, trust me. It is."

ABOUT THE AUTHOR

Susan Kiernan-Lewis lives in Ponte Vedra, Florida and writes mysteries and romantic suspense. Like many authors, Susan depends on the reviews and word of mouth referrals of her readers. If you enjoyed *Heartless*, please consider leaving a review saying so on Amazon.com, Barnesandnoble.com or Goodreads.com.
Check out Susan's website at susankiernanlewis.com and feel free to contact her at sanmarcopress@me.com.

Made in the USA
Monee, IL
25 April 2021